FLIRTING WITH GLOWSTICKS

Haylee Manda Reynolds

For the girls who see

themselves inside these pages

PART I

Age 16

Rory and I were soulmates.

At night, we threw glowsticks on top of buildings—neon secrets in the night, and then we cracked the rest open and painted our bodies lustrous.

"Are these toxic?" I asked.

He laughed. "Too late now."

The thing was, I didn't just like Rory. It wasn't enough that he was cute and funny with sky blue eyes. Or that he let me put seventeen SpongeBob Band-Aids on his face, or that he hid my keys in the fridge. It was the day he missed the bus, and I drove him home with a brand-new license in my red Volkswagen Beetle.

"Turn here," he said, as we were already passing his street, and I swerved—too late. In the opposite lane, a mother and her child screamed from the front seat of a minivan. I held my breath, bracing for the head-on collision. To kill a family at sixteen years old.

Rory's side of the car scraped against the guardrail as my hubcap rolled away in the rearview mirror. Somehow, I missed them, and in .2 seconds, life returned to normal. Like it didn't even happen. We drove to his house, and it was an inconsequential memory.

But my hands were shaking. Rory's back was straight as a board. My face—molten lava. He'd never ride with me again. Then he smiled, bright and easy, and asked, "Do you think this counts as a car accident?"

I was sixteen years old, eating dinner with Rory and his family, when his uncle looked at us in that way that uncles do, with an all-seeing wisdom that doesn't actually exist, and said, "It is scientifically proven that couples who look similar stay together and get married."

In my memory, there is a great round of applause, as if Rory had already asked me, and I said yes.

And then us, looking at each other, knowingly.

Yes. Deep in our hearts, *yes.*

That night, in the darkness of my bedroom, I wept, baffled at the explosion of emotion in my chest. The combination of me and Rory was a wildfire that made me feel happy and crazy and alive. To love and be loved was a miracle to me. But the only physical traits we shared were dirty blonde hair and big, dopey smiles. Rory had blue eyes and lanky skater boy limbs. I was a fleshy woman—my eyes, either orange or green.

In December, we played Truth or Dare with Rory's aunt, her baby rocking beside her on the floor. About as exciting as watching the bay freeze outside the window, until she dared me and Rory to jump in. The sky swirled with flurries. The wind was bitter cold, and we giggled, shivering in our long t-shirts and jeans. Then, on the count of three, we held hands and ran.

My body hit the water like a thousand needles. My hair turned to silk, slapping my face like a wet towel, as I rose to the surface and screamed. Rory's head burst out of the water, and he shook his hair like a dog.

Inside, I borrowed his clothes while he took a shower, and I pretended it wasn't all I'd ever wanted: to be warm and loved, to wear my boyfriend's gym shorts. "Truth or dare?" his aunt asked again, because we didn't have anything to talk about. I hugged his hoodie around me like a blanket.

"Truth."

"Do you really think you and Rory are going to make it?"

My heart stuttered like a butterfly on the interstate as she looked at me, like this was a test—like she knew something that I didn't.

"Yeah," my voice squeaked. "It's only two years. I love him."

"That's sweet."

I smiled like her words didn't make me wonder if that was stupid.

Then he walked into the room with messy shower hair and a gorgeous smile, and I thought, no. No, it's not stupid.

The week before Rory left, it snowed ferociously. In hot pink rainboots, I wore three pairs of socks, and I'll never forget standing in the freezing bay up to my shins, knowing. This moment—Rory and the untouched snow—the pure expanse of white, crystalline beach—him smiling at me with red lips, his hair speckled with falling snowflakes. The purity of desire.

The last hour was beautiful and desperate, and I tried not to look at the clock, but it was moving so damn fast. With only forty minutes left, I was logging every second, memorizing the texture of his hands—the temperature of his lips.

The inside of the house was relatively intact for a family that was moving to Tokyo in thirty-five minutes. Still, the tower of boxes kept growing in the driveway. His parents disappeared with his little sister, and I was too alive to be grateful.

Thirty. We spent our time laughing. Jokes that didn't make any sense. A tickle fight that ended in him curled up on the floor, begging for a breath. I loved his smile. And then my mom's green van was in the driveway, and there was no more time. I was kissing him through the window, one last tear-streaked kiss. My hands were in his greasy hair, and we were driving away. Goodbye, true love. Goodbye, beauty in the world. Goodbye, a life worth living forever and ever.

Had Rory stayed in Virginia Beach, we could have dated a few more months and watched our relationship disintegrate the old-fashioned way. Maybe some pent-up resentment that toxically seeped out over time, or a volcanic eruption of an argument that deemed us morally and rightfully unfit for one another. A sense of justice would be achieved. Order restored in the world.

Instead, we Skyped a couple times a week. His helicopter parents never left the room, and he whispered the terrible love letters.

The room was dark, and he was barely a shadow. I remembered the way he used to look at me, and my heart ached. There was no being with him anymore—no talking freely, no laughter.

The day before I broke up with him, I got his Valentine's Day package in the mail, with a stuffed heart that had arms to hug me. It was Hell. I wanted his arms to hug me. I was so tired of being sad, and I hated that I couldn't be with him. I hated that I loved him, and that I would stop loving him, and that ending it was the only way I knew how to be happy again.

What was love if it wasn't the great eternal truth of every girl's dreams? What was love if I'd found my soulmate, and then it ended, and it was nobody's fault?

True love, I thought, was supposed to be foolproof. Wasn't my parents'? Wasn't that how all the movies went? But my dreams were a hoax. True love came and went.

Age 14

Once upon a time, I imagined my story beginning the day I met my soulmate. But life is much more interesting than that. It started with me and my parents in Blue Rock. There are pictures of us on Dad's birthday. All of us wore alligator party hats—the kind that come out past your face and make it look like you're being eaten alive, or else you ripped off its jaw and put it on your head as a trophy. Anyway. We sat on the floor, and we trashed the living room with tissue paper—purple, blue, and pink—throwing it in the air and watching its slow descent onto the green shag carpet in front of the TV.

Mom was wearing jeans and a baggy gray t-shirt. Her chestnut brown hair was cut to her chin, and under the hat, she had the short bangs from the time she tried to cut them herself. Dad looked like he'd just woken up, in gym shorts and a plain black sweatshirt. He was tan and bald, with a big beard and bright blue eyes, and he and Mom were leaning into each other out of habit—or love.

At fourteen, I was full of funny faces, with long blonde hair, a tank top and pajama shorts. None of us had anything to prove then (except my hair, which I straightened). We were solid. We were happy. Life was good.

We lived in Cabin 18 at Blue Rock State Park—the opposite of our life in Connecticut, where we'd lived in Mom's dream house—white with blue shutters (like *The Notebook*), two stories, and a breakfast nook that looked out over the backyard.

The day my dad asked us if we wanted to move, I was in eighth grade. The three of us were sprawled out on my parents' quilted double bed, leaning crooked on our elbows, bellies aching with laughter.

"Seriously, though. Should I apply for the job?"

Dad had earned a bachelor's degree, scrubbed toilets for minimum wage, and graduated from Police Academy—all for this moment—the opportunity to move to the heart of Virginia (aka the middle of nowhere) and live in a 500-square-foot cabin meant for camping. It was absurd, and it sounded like an adventure.

I don't remember officially deciding—just Dad saying, "It'll be a lot less space. We'll be kind of on top of each other."

And me giggling, "Like we are right now?"

And that was that move's Tripod meeting, just laughing and dreaming together.

The weekend of the interview, we spent that first night in our future house playing board games around a kitchen table straight out of the center of a tree. Only when they started falling did we notice hundreds of orange ladybugs clustered around the ceiling fan. Over our heads and into our hair, they dropped like tiny skydivers, the beat of their wings blaring in our ears. It was so loud, between the buzzing and the screaming and our laughter bouncing off the orange cedar walls.

We laughed until we cried, and when we got home to our real suburban life, we prayed that Dad would get the job.

The ladybugs followed us back up to New England, little messengers crawling up the walls and infiltrating my dreams, walking with tiny pitter-patter feet across my homework. Finding me at school. Landing on my arm. On the day they heard the news, Mom picked me up from school early. She sat me down on a bench in the lobby, and I was trying to figure out who had died, when she looked at me with her big brown eyes before practically whispering, "Chloe, he got the job."

Dad was officially a Park Ranger.

Even better, there was a girl named Alex who also lived in a cabin at the park, and she was in the same grade as me. In Connecticut, I didn't have any close girlfriends. I was too quiet. Terrified, actually, of the consequences of speaking. Like the only way to not say the wrong thing was to never talk at all—or to never say anything that could reveal my thoughts or feelings.

There was this girl in my math class who tried to be my friend once. We sat beside each other every single day without having a real conversation until three-quarters of the way through the year, she sat down beside me with a huge smile and said, "Hi!"

"Hiii, how are youuu?" I asked robotically.

"No," she said, "Talk to me like we're friends."

My head jerked, as I looked at her properly for the first time. She had black hair with brown roots and piercing sea green eyes.

"I am," I said, but it was more of a question.

I hoped that in my new life, things would be different. I wanted friends, but more than that, I wanted a best friend, and I thought Alex might be the One.

We moved to Blue Rock, Virginia at the end of summer, and meeting Alex was average in that we didn't hit it off and we didn't not hit it off. We didn't know each other; we didn't know ourselves, and we were both going into our first year of high school. At Open House, I followed her around our new school while she introduced me to all her friends. One long performance.

"Hi, I'm Chloe."

"Hi, I'm Chloe."

"Hi, I'm Chloe."

And all the people, in my face and happy to meet me.

"Hi, my name's Breanna, and I'm CRAZY!"

And I met my teachers, who required a calm reverence, and saw the classrooms where I'd be living, and opened and closed a locker for the first time. I met Ezra, Alex's best friend in the whole world who I was supposed to love, and I was hyperaware that there was no spark or chemistry in the initial hi-nice-to-meet-you conversation. And then I went back to the car and cried alone in the backseat while my parents waited outside. Nothing was wrong, and they knew it. Everything was just so new.

It was my first week of school. I was standing alone in the bus loop, clutching the straps of my backpack, wondering if I'd missed the bus. That's when Ezra appeared, wearing ripped black jeans and a faux leather jacket, and I didn't know whether to wave or smile or ignore him. Because I didn't know if he even remembered who I was. Then his face lit up when he saw me, and somehow, with his big brown eyes and genuine smile, he made me feel at home, waiting for the bus that was already gone.

We laughed together as the last bus drove away.

"I guess I'll call my parents," I said.

"Yeah, I better go too. My mom's been waiting in the parking lot for like fifteen minutes." It was so like him, to be so kind and gentle and selfish, all at once.

Alex was the common link between me and Ezra. They were best friends, and eventually, Alex and I became best friends too. Still, it took time. Like siblings, we grew into each other through proximity. Every morning, we waited at the bus stop together, clenching our jackets in the dark. She fell asleep beside me on the bus with her mouth hanging open, head flopping dangerously towards me and the seat in front of us, while I watched the colors change from night to day through the window.

On the weekends, we spent as much time as we could together, as there was nothing to do and nowhere to go—except

for when I socially maxed out, and I'd tell her I had a head-
ache so I could sit in my room with the door closed and read.
Otherwise, we did everything together: made barbeque
chicken and pineapple pizza from scratch, devoted entire Sat-
urdays to the art of shuffling cards, perfected the application
of liquid eyeliner, scrunched our hair with mousse, and tanned
on the porch until our skin peeled white again.

When William Gardner asked me out, I said yes, though I'd never thought of him in that way before. Alex had told me about him over the summer. They'd had "a thing" in middle school, which meant hugging and being extra awkward around each other. That didn't change much in ninth grade. William and I held hands standing in the lobby with our friends, and we kissed for the first time with our backpacks on in the bus loop—my first kiss.

His breath smelled like cheese, and I was disappointed. I liked having a hand to hold but not the smell of William's breath in my mouth. The truth is, we didn't like each other. We were just bored, and he broke up with me three weeks later in that same spot with a serious, empathetic look on his face.

"I think it would be better if we were just friends," he said softly.

Without skipping a beat, I shrugged and said, "Yeah, me too." His face glitched as I walked away. My ego was hurt, but I didn't show it, and it paid off. Everyone made fun of William that week instead of me.

The first time Ezra invited me over to his house, he and Alex sat me down in the living room and played old VCR tapes of "when Will used to be cool." In Ezra's grainy, home-made horror film, William humped a big red truck wearing stilettos, a black dress, and a tangled bleach blonde wig.

"Will and I used to be friends," Ezra explained. "But then he got boring."

That night, we made Jiffy Pop over the stove (which took forever) and watched as many scary movies as we could before falling asleep. They were awful—*thank freaking Jesus*—as Alex would have said, since I liked to sleep and not lie awake in bed with my eyes open, scanning the room for demons.

The Headless Horseman, for example, was less of a movie and more like two hours of watching a headless shadow ride around in the distant, sunsetting hills. It was kind of boring to me, but Alex and I snuggled up on the recliner eating popcorn, and I loved my new friends.

Christopher and Alex broke up two weeks before the park's Fall Festival. With greasy hair and a spidery mustache, Christopher wasn't the most attractive. But he was always my favorite, because he was funny and I loved to laugh. Anyway, they'd only ever hugged. Neither of them seemed upset by it. And he kept his promise to be zombies with us for the Haunted Hayride.

"So what exactly do we do?" I asked Dad, and he shrugged.

"Just act like zombies."

Easy enough. Alex, Christopher, and I ruffled each other's hair and dressed up in ripped, ragged clothes covered in fake blood. While we waited for the tractor, we turned like skewers around the fire pit, warming our hands and then our backs and our hands again.

When we finally saw it—the Haunted Hayride—dragging a trailer full of people, we panicked and jumped around the fire, making caveman noises. Nothing to do with zombies actually, because we'd forgotten to make a plan.

When Alex went inside to use the bathroom, Christopher and I discovered the glowsticks and chucked them at each other as hard as we could. The plastic stung my legs through my jeans, and I liked that he didn't go easy on me. That was the moment—as Alex's shadow appeared in the distance—I realized that I liked Christopher as more than a friend.

At Ezra's Halloween party, I wore my first "sexy" Halloween costume—a black flapper dress with leather boots and a push-up bra that almost gave me cleavage. When I stood on my toes to kiss Christopher for the first time under the orange and black streamers, I pretended not to see his friends watching from across the room. But they were impossible to miss, their mouths hanging open, teeth glowing green under the blacklights.

Alex's sexy zombie costume didn't go over as well because of the bloody rip across her stomach. "Gross," Christopher whispered, for my benefit.

His friend pretended to gag, and I rolled my eyes.

"Don't be mean," I said, in case she'd noticed. Then I shoved Christopher into his friend. He pushed me back, and we were flirting.

I was winning the impossible game. I was fun. I was pretty. I was kind of standing up for my friend.

After the party, the boys went home, and the girls spent the night at Ezra's house, eating peanut butter pumpkins in our pajamas.

"Truth or dare?" Ezra asked Alex.

"Truth."

He thought for a second—not too long—and then smiled deviously.

"How do you feel about Chloe going out with Christopher?"

I think I stopped breathing. Alex sat on the floor between her friends from middle school, and I looked down at her from the recliner. No one spoke. She looked at the carpet, then at me, and then Ezra. Her friends watched—horror-struck, excited. Time froze, like I was in an actual horror movie. But I didn't have anything to say or offer.

I guess I wanted to know, too.

"It's—fine," she said finally, with an inflection that sounded like a lie. "I'm fine with it."

But I was only relieved when it was the next person's turn. And then that person asked a question. And someone made out with the wall, and Ezra touched nipples with Zoe. And Alex was laughing. And maybe she and everyone else had forgotten.

I wish I could say that I was a chicks before dicks type of girl, but I wasn't. In ninth grade, I was finally making moves towards falling in love. For the first time in my life, I felt pretty. I felt desirable, and the boys I liked, liked me back.

Christopher wasn't my first love, but he was the first boyfriend I had real chemistry with. We played off each other's jokes. We made each other laugh, and we both liked roller skating. It was enough—until a month in, when he decided it wasn't.

What made it so awkward was that, on the days I went roller skating with Christopher, Alex always came with me. It was perfect. Alex and I rented the grimy roller skates with rickety neon orange wheels, and on our favorite songs, we held hands and danced across the black glistening floor. Christopher skated circles around us, making us laugh and teasing when we tripped. With one arm wrapped around my waist and the other ready to catch me when I fell, he taught me how to skate like I was flying. I alternated between my boyfriend and my bestie, and it was seamless. My life was like a movie.

Until Christopher wanted me to make out with him, and I didn't want to. Because I didn't know how. And I didn't want to learn at the Riverside Sk8way with Alex and everyone else watching. But he didn't ask what I wanted. He got me up against the wall—stuck between two wooden benches. Then he leaned in, parted his lips, and waited. When I didn't put my tongue in his mouth, he put his hands in the back pockets of my jeans. He didn't care that we were in public. He didn't care that no one had ever touched me like that or that I didn't want to be touched like that. But the word—*no*—was stuck in my throat. I wanted to disappear, but I was stuck on my skates, suffocating in the hot air between us—the smell of Axe and sweat.

Finally, I turned my face away from him, and there was Alex, watching us with sunken shoulders. Her face telling me everything as she skated away. That Christopher was her ex. That I'd turned her into a third wheel. That I was a bad friend. And this was all my fault.

Christopher's older brother skated by then—what else was there to do in Blue Rock?

"Gettin' a little somethin' extra, bud?" he shouted.

"More like not enough," Christopher frowned, letting me go. Then he skated away, too.

That was Friday. Saturday was the worst. I spent all day lying on the couch, listening to sad girl music and staring up at the ceiling—the music only making me sadder as my head spun like—*Why am I such a bad friend? How could I have done that to her? And why couldn't I just make out with him and be a good girlfriend?*

But I didn't have any answers to those questions, so I just sunk deeper into my feelings, getting quieter and quieter until it was finally late enough to sleep. Just as I was about to melt into bed and disappear into my dreams, my dad knocked on the door, and I mumbled for him to come in.

"What's wrong, buddy?" he asked gently, walking into the room. He was just trying to be nice, but I was too tired to care about his feelings.

"I literally just want this day to be over."

"Is it about Christopher?"

"I'm *not* going to talk about this with you," I said, welcoming the rush of anger as he sat next to me on the bed.

"I know," he said. "I know. But—I mean—I've been a teenage boy before, is the thing."

"And?"

"Do you want my advice?"

Of course I wanted his advice if it included insider perspective on the male brain. But I wasn't about to admit it.

"Fine."

His whole body relaxed.

"Sometimes, when boys don't get what they want, they act sad. Then, if that doesn't work, they act mad." Then he paused for a second. "But it's all just a show, to make you do what they want."

I smiled a little.

"Really?" I asked, and he nodded.

"You just got to be yourself, girl."

Then I rolled my eyes. "Way to ruin it, Dad."

Still, I went to bed feeling like maybe I wasn't such a jerk, after all. Christopher broke up with me anyway a couple of weeks later, and I found Alex in the bus loop so I could hug her and cry uncontrollably. I wasn't in love, but I was still heartbroken.

"Luke," Alex whispered into her phone.

"Yes?"

He was a boy I knew from middle school.

"I am your father."

Then we plastered our hands over our mouths to stop the giggles from coming while we waited for his response.

"Who is this?" Luke asked. There were people in the background—guys. They were having a sleepover too, and we didn't hang up.

"Your mother," I croaked.

Then someone shouted, "Give me the phone!"

The next boy made it his mission to figure us out, and we played twenty questions until it got boring, and Alex revealed herself. Then they stayed on the phone for another hour, while I cut out models from magazines and taped them to her turquoise walls, wondering if she would ever hang up.

Alex got Kevin's number, and talking to him became her new favorite thing. She talked to him after school, when I was at her house, in my room, on my bed, and the day her mom drove us three hours to the mall. We were supposed to be shopping for Ezra's birthday party. It was supposed to be fun. Then Kevin called, and she didn't even talk to me the whole time. It was like shopping by myself.

I found my outfit in about five minutes. After that, there was nothing left to do except drink my mocha Frappuccino and listen to her side of the conversation. But half the time, they weren't even saying anything. It would have been the same conversation if Kevin had hung up on her, and she was just holding the phone up to her ear. It was like she was purposely ignoring me.

"Why are you even on the phone?" I whispered, and she shooed my voice away.

"There's a sale going on at Victoria's Secret," Alex said to Kevin, stealing a sip of my drink.

I'd never been inside Victoria's Secret. The models in the advertisements freaked me out—like they were daring me to look at their boobs, and it was my job to walk by with my eyes glued to the floor. "I don't know. What do you think I'd look good in?" she asked, and I was so annoyed.

But I thought of Christopher at the roller-skating rink— Alex skating away with her sad shoulders, and I swallowed the ball of fury in my chest. Pushed the raging boredom all the way down. Pretended that I didn't mind being a third wheel to Alex and her phone. And I tried to not be mad at her.

Friends don't get mad at each other, I thought. *I'm nice.*

I'm nice, I thought, sampling the cherry blossom lotion in Bath & Body Works.

I'm nice, I'm nice, I'm nice.

Then her mom picked us up and asked if we had fun, and I smiled and showed her my clothes.

I couldn't tell you what Ezra's favorite Lady Gaga song was. But if I were forced to guess, I'd say *Paparazzi,* the song I secretly despised the most—because the music video was seven minutes long, and he loved watching it.

The Fame was the album of our lives that year, and it was playing the night of my first photoshoot, when Ezra transformed me and Alex into supermodels using the clothes we'd brought from home—jeans and hoodies, zipped down to our cleavage (which for me, was mostly imagined). Under the house, Ezra crawled between the water pipes with a flashlight in one hand and his camera bag flung over his shoulder. Alex and I followed on our hands and knees, trying not to get our clothes dirty.

When it was my turn to model, Alex held the flashlight while Ezra gave orders he'd learned from *America's Next Top Model,* to smize or pout or put my arm up around that pipe and position my hand "like it's a little spider"—all to the soundtrack of Lady Gaga—*Starstruck, Poker Face,* and that one about the disco stick.

But even with simple commands, he couldn't teach me how to stop being awkward. Alex's pink lips were naturally plump and pouty—her green eyes intuitively fierce, while the instruction to smize only made my eyes—soft and hazel— twitch.

The Fame was the album of our lives and the theme of Ezra's birthday party. Silver paper lanterns hung from the ceiling of the detached garage, with complementing hues of silver, purple and blue all around the room. He built a photo backdrop based off the album cover and set up a projector to play music videos during the party.

My entire outfit was from Hot Topic. For some reason—maybe because I was secretly pissed—I went rock 'n' roll that day at the mall, with checkered pants, a purple Jimi Hendrix shirt, and thick black eyeliner all the way around. Ezra gave me piggyback rides to the food table, and I ate meatballs and chocolate covered pretzels over his shoulder between rounds of dancing my brains out.

When *Brown Eyes* started playing, I looked around for Alex so we could slow dance silly together like zombie centaurs or something. But when I found her, she was already dancing with Christopher. His arms were wrapped around her waist. Her hands dangled loose behind his neck, and everything went slow motion for me.

She smiled at him, blushing, and I could hear my heartbeat, like my sadness had a pulse. I wanted to cry and explode and never talk to anyone again. I had to go. I couldn't stay. I didn't want to face her and the rest of the party, pretending all night that everything was fine, because it wasn't. Nothing was fine.

"I'll be right back," I said, to no one in particular.

I walked out of the garage into the chilly night air—*don't cry, don't cry, don't cry*. Through the wet grass. Into the house and up the stairs. Straight for Alex's iPod. Then I crawled under the covers in all my clothes, and I listened to *When It Rains* by Paramore on repeat until I fell asleep.

"Chloeeee."

I woke up to Alex leaning over me, whispering in a sweet, cooing voice, "Chloee, wake up." Her brown hair was silky against my bare arm, and I could smell her conditioner, or her lotion, or whatever it was that made her smell like vanilla all the time. It was nauseating.

I didn't know if she'd meant anything by dancing with Christopher—only that I would have done the same to her. She'd finally settled the score. For every time I'd dated one of her exes or turned her into a third wheel, we were finally even.

She poked my shoulder like it was all just a joke. "Come back to the party," she said. "It's Ezra's birthday."

But there was no way I could show my face at that party again. So, I kept my eyes closed and pretended I was still asleep until she left.

The next morning, life continued. No one said anything about it. Nothing happened between Alex and Christopher, and I didn't carry a grudge. I was just glad that things went back to normal so easily.

When summer hit, Ezra's parents opened up the pool. We stayed up 'til four and slept in 'til noon, and every day was the weekend. The first time Ezra and I both woke up before Alex, I stayed in bed a little longer, waiting for her to open her eyes. The problem was, besides the time I'd missed the bus, I'd never been alone with Ezra. How would I find the things to say, with Alex drooling, practically dead in the cot upstairs? What if Ezra saw the real, quiet me, and he thought I was boring?

But eventually, I had to pee, and Ezra caught me coming out of the bathroom.

"Want to go to the pool?" he smiled.

I bought myself time, jumping off the diving board and doing handstands—anything to get my head under the water. When Ezra showed me how to do a backflip, I smiled and laughed in all the right places. I got water up my nose on the way down and laughed at myself while I choked and noticed how much cooler he was than me. And even though I kept looking up towards the bedroom window, mentally invoking her, Alex didn't come.

When I got cold, I climbed the metal ladder on the deep end and sat down on the side of the pool with a green and blue frog towel wrapped around my shoulders. I was wearing a swimsuit that felt awkward on my body—a green and yellow bikini that made my soft, white belly look like cottage cheese.

I covered up with a towel as Ezra pushed his way up and out of the water to sit beside me.

Ezra was so much fun. He was smart. He was creative, and he was the funniest person I'd ever met. When would I give myself away, that I was actually quiet and boring and not fun to talk to at all?

My swimsuit bottoms stuck to the concrete every time I shifted, and I kept looking down to make sure my pubes weren't showing. When my body felt drier than my towel, I checked again, then tossed my towel aside and laid back in the sun. Alex wasn't coming.

Ezra balled his towel into a pillow under his head, his long legs dangling in the water, and the moments between us passed by slowly, in a "sitting on the beach" kind of way. The sun baked the chlorine into my skin. I felt dry and crusty and maybe even a little relaxed. Even without Alex, he made me laugh without trying, and for some reason, he laughed at my jokes, too. Besides, he really did talk enough for the two of us. During a short silence, I started to panic, but it turned out Ezra was just working up the nerve to tell me he liked Brendan McCoy.

It was the moment when both of our lives changed forever. I shouted, "WHAT!?"

Oh, I knew he was gay, though it was a secret, and he'd never explicitly told me—but I couldn't believe his taste. Brendan sat in front of me in History class. We flirted, but he needed deodorant.

"Yes, God!" Ezra groaned, his head leaning back into the sun. "Those muscles!"

Brendan was bulky. "And he does have a nice smile," I said. Goofy, but adorable. I thought of Brendan in class, talking when the teacher was talking, and ripping paper into thousands of tiny pieces that fell onto the floor when he stood up to go to the bathroom.

"He goes to the bathroom like every five minutes!" I couldn't help but laugh.

We talked for hours, as he told me the struggles of inevitably having a crush on a straight boy. I told him in turn about my latest soccer boy crush, which would evaporate by the end of the week. Though it was apparently so obvious that Ezra had already known.

There were moments of silence, but it was nothing too awkward. Eventually we did get bored. Though it had nothing to do with me. It was a long time that we'd spent talking, with the shadows moving across the pavement, and we decided to finally go wake up Alex. The day was ordinary, but it was the day when Ezra and I became best friends.

In June, Alex and Ezra stayed at the cabin, and we spent the morning walking aimlessly around the park. Even though it was eighty degrees, I wore hot pink rainboots with shorts, rose-colored sunglasses shaped like lips, and an oversized hoodie. Ezra took pictures of our shadows on the road and Alex and I climbing trees before we discovered an abandoned house in the woods that Ezra swore was haunted.

Through a rotting door hanging from rusty hinges, we found dirt-streaked walls and sunlight filtering through a film of dust. We tiptoed across the floor, around trash and broken dishes, each in our own direction, as my heart pounded in my chest. But I wasn't worried about getting caught. I was afraid of ghosts—lurking in the closets, and in the bedrooms in the back of the house, behind the walls and doors, and all the places we couldn't see.

A layer of thick dust coated a black piano in the corner of the living room, and I whisper-yelled at Ezra as he pressed a key, out of tune and spooky.

"Don't touch it!" I said, already creeped out as I picked up a piece of broken porcelain and put it in my pocket as a souvenir.

Then Ezra grabbed his forehead and squinted like he was in pain.

"There's something here," he said. Not someone. Something.

Alex and I locked eyes.

"You're just trying to scare us," she said.

"Yeah," Ezra said, ignoring her. "Definitely some paranormal activity here." He was always claiming to have psychic powers.

"Oh, God, it's so strong," he moaned, rubbing his temples, and even though I had a feeling he was lying, Alex and I bolted out of the house. Ezra rushed behind us, and we raced back to the street, breathless and giggling.

Before dinner, we rode bikes twelve miles down to the gas station and back. Ezra and I made a game out of going as fast as we could and then slowing down for Alex, red-faced and irritated about God knows what—probably us leaving her, but we didn't care.

The road was gray with the shade and the lush green trees towering over us, and I remember Ezra's laugh as he zoomed down a hill with his red lumberjack flannel flying out behind him, his legs spread open to the wind. Uphill, my feet pounded into the pedals, blood rushing through my veins. The wind whipped through my hair, tangling my curls and matting them together, and I felt beautiful and free.

That summer, I spent time with my parents without noticing them. They were watching me grow up; I wasn't watching them. They were always the same to me—just Mom and Dad.

Dad worked out with his friends in the morning before work, and he made chicken breast for dinner so many times that I never wanted chicken again. When he lost forty pounds, he looked the same to me, except for when he shaved his beard. Then his entire head was tan and bald, besides the little blonde elephant hairs that sometimes stuck up on top.

Since we lived in the middle of nowhere, Mom got a boring desk job, and she sometimes complained about her coworkers, who were bitchy and talked too much, until Dad requested that we eat dinner without having to hear about Julie tonight. Mom bought a new shirt every time she didn't feel like doing laundry, and every few months, she'd buy a new workout outfit to motivate herself to start running, even though she never did.

There's a story Dad used to tell—so many times I can see it, as if I'm there, sitting next to Mom on the picnic table while she drinks her glass of wine (red, even in the summer). In reality, I wasn't there. I was away. It's dusk—summertime without me at Cabin 18.

When Dad gets home from work, Mom is sitting on the picnic table beside an empty bottle of Cabernet.

"James," she says, before he's even out of the truck. She has that silly drunk face where the corners of her mouth turn down, like when she's sleeping. "Look at that little cloud."

"What cloud?" he asks, sitting down next to her. The periwinkle sky is clear that night.

"Right there," she says. "The only cloud in the sky."

"Where?" He squints his eyes. He can't see it.

"Jesus Christ, James! It's right there! In the middle of the sky!"

"Amber!" He laughs so hard he yells, "That's the MOON!"

We all laughed, every time he told it. It was so her—so us, since I was turning out to be just like her. And Dad—he always roared at the end of the story, like it was happening for the first time. I didn't know it then. Maybe she didn't even know it, but I'd think about that story a lot within the next few years.

Mama was bored.

From the pool, I smelled like chlorine in the daytime, and at night, I came out of the shower smelling like liquid gold—the same body wash every time—and iron, the smell of the water as it poured from the shower head like a warm rain—with very low pressure.

Ezra didn't shower, so he smelled like him—and something about the forest.

Malik, Nicolas, and Olivia started hanging out with us more when their parents made friends with Ezra's parents, and every weekend became a party.

Malik was two years younger than us, but anyone would have guessed younger. In eighth grade, he was four feet tall with baby fat and a big toothy smile, and he almost never stopped talking about Pokémon—to me, specifically, because I was the only one who would listen.

"So everything basically makes sense," he'd start, as I'm trying to eat a slice of pizza. "Like electric types are stronger than ice types because fire burns ice, right? But water type Pokémon don't do a whole lot against earth type. You see what I mean? Water basically feeds earth, so I always choose fire Pokémon. That's the smart thing to do. Anyone who doesn't choose fire is an idiot, hands down." Then he'd pause. "Plus, I just like Charmander."

Malik was a little annoying, but he was fun—especially since Alex was getting boring. She disappeared for hours at a time to talk on the phone, and it was weird to listen to—equal parts dull and fascinating. I'd sit beside her on the steps of the porch or poke my head out the door to ask her a question, and she'd talk about a toad in the grass with a voice that sounded more like phone sex. Then, when I left, there would be phone sex. I knew because she told me, all the time, with her green eyes like fire, more excited than I'd ever seen her before: "And then he asked me, *What would we do if you were here?*"

I'm not going to lie and say I didn't pay attention for educational purposes. But for the most part, the rest of us weren't interested. Olivia didn't say much, but she smiled every time someone said anything inappropriate, and I never saw her without her Kermit the Frog hat. Plus, we bonded over *Yo Gabba Gabba!* because we had the same level of appreciation for insanity. The scenes were short and sweet and disconnected—kids dancing across psychedelic backdrops; weird live-action monsters that hobbled instead of walked; and my favorite side story, Super Martian Robot Girl, who was short and green with long wiry antennas.

At the beach, a giant lobster drank civilian juice boxes, and Super Martian Robot Girl saved the day by explaining that he (the lobster) was just thirsty—which apparently made everything okay. The plotlines were horrifying. Somehow, that made it better.

"Why are we watching this?" Nicolas groaned.

Good question.

Nicolas was a freshman, but he looked more like a man than a boy. When he was curled up on the couch, you could almost trace the lines of his muscles with your eyes.

Ezra snapped back like a feral cat, "Shut up, Nikki. You're just jealous cause Super Martian Robot Girl is ten billion times cooler than you'll ever be in your sad, straight life."

And then Nicolas smiled that mischievous, tight-lipped straight boy smile, and nothing changed, and everything was perfect.

I discovered that I liked coloring that year when we found the crayons in the closet, and I started drawing my own characters and coloring entire pages red. Before that, I thought I wasn't patient enough for art. I didn't pick the right colors. I didn't color in the lines. The crayons broke between my fingers, and everything Alex made was perfect. Everything Alex made looked like an advertisement for coloring books. But Ezra taped our pictures to the wall and called it "Art" and we created a tapestry of color and chaos.

The driveway to Ezra's house was long and narrow, with blue-gray pavement and a hill with the best cellphone reception on the property. All the way from the 55-mph backroad to the white house at the bottom of the hill, there was a ranch-style fence with electric silver wires hanging suspended between the rungs. The house was surrounded by rolling hills of grass in every direction, with the cows huddled in their own corner of the pasture.

"Do you eat them?" I asked Ezra once.

"Oh, they're not ours," he told me. "They're Old Richard Young's." And then he explained the deal Richard had with his dad—why the cattle were on the land, and how you could tell by their color, whether they were beef or dairy cows.

And I said, "Oh," and immediately forgot.

Ezra was born and raised in Blue Rock, and just like everyone else, he knew every person in the county by name. He always talked about them like I knew them too, even though I didn't know anybody.

The cattle that lived on the property were black or ginger, and whenever they managed to eat all or most of the grass in that part of the pasture, Old Richard herded them into another section of land. For me, the cows were an essential part of the sleepover experience. Just on the other side of the fence, picking their noses with their long pink tongues, they looked like big pets that would probably snuggle.

The day Ezra and I decided to go on a walk, the cows were far across the pasture—just dots on a hill, and our minds kept turning towards the electric fence.

How bad could it really hurt? we wondered. Could it really keep the cows out—these thousand-pound creatures, with hooves and four stomachs? A wire?

We wondered, and before we knew it, we were lying next to each other on our bellies, our legs on the pavement and our torsos in the wiry, golden grass, experimenting. I was giggling, holding a small stick to a blade of grass that was touching the wire directly. I didn't know much, but I knew that electricity sometimes traveled, and I hoped that through all the layers—me and the stick and the grass—it wouldn't travel now.

Mine and Ezra's shoulders were touching, and he watched me, smiling and curious, with his shaggy hair blowing in the bitter wind. When nothing happened, he laid his head on the ground and laughed. "What are we even doing?"

Step two was to see if the electricity could shock us directly through the grass.

"You do it," I said, nudging him with my elbow.

With his eyes squeezed shut, he poked the grass and pulled his finger back as fast as he could.

"What happened?" I asked, my eyes wide with excitement. "Did you feel anything?"

"I don't know," he said, slowly touching his finger to the grass again and holding it there. "It's kind of…tingly."

"Should we go under?"

"I don't know," he said.

Then I smiled and said, "Come on."

I shimmied under the fence with Ezra right behind me.

"We weren't electrocuted!" we cheered, dusting off our jeans on the other side.

Then we started walking, since that had been the plan all along, arm in arm or beside each other with our hands shoved in our pockets.

"Are we allowed to be in here?" I asked Ezra, suddenly remembering his parents. But he waved a hand towards the house.

"We said we were going on a walk, didn't we?"

Ezra and I talked some, but it was mostly just being together—tromping through the grass—frosty like snow, as it crunched under our feet.

Sometimes we held hands, which felt good and natural, and I loved him in a way that was both platonic and boundless—as grounding and expansive as the fields, which were different than I'd expected. Every few minutes, we'd be walking along, avoiding another hard, dried-up cow pie, when we were faced with another electric fence or an old rusty gate to climb.

It wasn't deliberate, the decision to walk towards the cows, but eventually, as we grew closer, I was happy to be near them. In that moment, they felt like my friends. But once Ezra and I crawled into the same section as them and stood up on their territory, I started to sweat. Cattle are really big, I noticed, grabbing Ezra's arm. Ezra was skinny, but he was a foot taller than me, and my only feeling of safety. I didn't know what the animals might do up close—if they liked me back, or if I was just imagining our friendship.

But it was an adventure, with the cows and Ezra and the great expanse of the Earth. So, we kept walking, right into the center of the field, in the middle of the herd, which was spread out, grazing—further apart than they'd looked in the distance.

I was scared but happy—avoiding the steaming hot piles of dung—all the way up to my ankles, if I'd have stepped in one. But I didn't. I was careful, looking down at the ground as I walked, when beside me, Ezra stopped.

"Oh God," he whispered.

I looked up, and we were surrounded—stopped in our tracks, outnumbered and outsmarted. The giant beasts, shaggy and terrifying, had formed a perfect circle around us.

They could kill us, I thought, as a young black cow packed its hoof against the ground, huffing. I looked up at Ezra's profile, beautiful and angular, and I thought, *We could die.*

"It's a bull," he said, his voice wavering with fear. "A teenager," and I squeezed his hand, his knuckles bony against my soft thumbprint. I thought of the way dogs bark when you look them in the eye, and I whispered, "Don't look at it."

But it was hard not to. Its nose was towards the ground, and its giant black eyes were glaring right at us. I'd seen that posture before, in other animals—in movies, and I knew what it meant. That bull was preparing to charge. Slowly, we moved away from it without speaking, towards a small gap in the circle, and my heart beat faster than it ever had in my life.

After many seconds of shuffling our feet, afraid to run yet fearing for our lives, we made it out of the circle of imminent death, and the cattle started eating grass again, like they do in cartoons or when they're not trying to kill you.

But only when we were on the other side of the electric fence did we scream, laughing hysterically, fired up at being alive.

"Those bitches are crazier than they look!" Ezra giggled, catching his breath, and I agreed. Crazier, indeed.

They say that your first true love will always have a special place in your heart, but I was confused about what that meant for me. Who *was* my first true love?

And what makes love true? Is it something that must be spoken? Does it have to be reciprocated? (Not that you could ever know.) And if your first love is a jerk, can you just call your second love your first *true* love, because the feeling of being held and loved and reciprocated in your affection somehow makes your love more "true"?

But if I'm objective enough, the answer is obvious. In my sophomore year of high school, I fell in love with Ezra—deeply, in a way that felt explosive and soul-baring. It happened gradually, just as our friendship had evolved at a slow and steady pace. Then, all of a sudden, I loved him. I needed him, and there was the feeling that if he wasn't in my life, my soul would literally die.

Of course, I didn't *tell him* this. He was *gay*. He liked *boys*.

Still, we became inseparable. We walked arm in arm down the hallways of the high school, leaning into each other in our laughing and falling into hysterics, and if I was lucky, on the weekends, he would sleep in the same bed as me. I can't remember a time when I wasn't touching him or wanting to. And I *knew* that Alex knew. When she cuddled with him on the couch, smiling innocently at me. When she tucked a brunette curl behind his ear, flirting with him. Holding that over me.

Ezra and I were best, best friends who brought out the crazy in each other—which was, I believed, the highest truth. And we adored each other in all of our most monstrous qualities. I loved his power and charisma, the mystery that was the mind of artistic genius. Though I wouldn't admit to myself that these qualities also drove me insane—how he could turn a situation in his favor with one sentence. And even when I knew I was being manipulated, I followed him. It was, after all, completely and totally Ezra, and I loved him down to his core.

There was no sex, and I didn't need it back then. I felt a deep resistance to getting physical with another person—an inner knowing that life would become more complicated then—that in the physical manifestation of my complete and total vulnerability, I would be at another's mercy. And no boy I knew deserved that.

With Ezra, there was no pressure or performance. There were no words that I could say to him that would make any sense of my feelings, and it was everything. He was everything I'd ever wanted in a lover.

Please, then? Can I just choose Ezra as my first true love? Do we *really* have to go into Fenix—and sex? Or can we just skip ahead to snuggling with Ezra on the carpet, watching *Harry Potter* while he hand-fed me grass-flavored jellybeans?

Please?

But I guess it happens to all of us.

Ezra had warned me, before Fenix and I were "official." It was a free day in gym, when the straight boys did real things like play basketball or lift weights, and us girls sat on the shiny orange bleachers and gossiped. Ezra and I sat at the very top, just the two of us, surrounded by the school flags, all blue and gold and dusty. I was telling him about this boy I met. He was a senior. His name was Fenix.

Ezra was quieter than usual, hunched over and pensive, when he looked at me with gentle eyes and said, slowly, "Listen. I know Hannah McClendon, his ex-girlfriend." He looked out over the basketball court and all its moving pieces—boys pulling lay-ups, a soccer game played with a dodgeball out of bounds, and the gym teacher, yawning and looking at his watch—and then back at me. "She told me they had *sex*. Like, a lot."

His eyes were wide, like he wanted answers from me. So, I took a deep breath, and I made a choice.

I said, "I trust him."

I met Fenix Adler in the spring of sophomore year. "Adler means eagle in German," he explained. He sure did love talking about himself.

It was the year of infinite bomb threats—long, leisurely days sweating in the football stands, half-anticipating an explosion from the building where we spent our lives. I watched the school across the field, wondering absent-mindedly how the bricks would react to a bomb. Would they hold their own or explode outwards? I hoped for fire.

I can't say I was as afraid as I should have been. No homework. No tests. Just a mob of teenagers, climbing across the hot, blinding bleachers, looking for our friends and waiting for the next round of frosty water bottles—courtesy of the teachers. Our lives were in their hands. Yet somehow, they didn't exist. For once, their power was undermined—their lesson plans shot to Hell.

The day I met Fenix was a bomb threat too, but since it was raining, they just sent us to the gym and told us to stay with our class. I guess they figured we'd all die together.

Fenix was six feet tall with gray eyes and a sharp, angular face. That day, his long brown hair hung loose over his shoulders, and somehow, in the sweaty gym, we ended up in a game of checkers. He sat above me in the stands—two spaces, with the black and red checkerboard resting between us, and I remember the way he made me blush—teasing me harshly in a way that only teenage boys can do. And I—violently shoving my hair behind my ears.

Afterwards, I was desperately hungry for Fenix's attention. He was in my art class—always had been. But after he beat me in checkers, things were different. We ignored each other the entire period, and when the bell rang, he sauntered over to talk to me—real relaxed. It must have been hard, with his long legs, to appear to be walking slowly. I pretended not to see him, like I really cared about how my backpack was organized. Until he was right there, clean-smelling and brilliant, with unwrinkled clothes and a crooked, boyish smile.

There were lots of hugs—step one in the elaborate dating game. His arms were long, like tentacles, and they wrapped around me again and again. It was like a glimpse into my future, when the guys were more like men than boys, and he felt warm, and strong, and safe.

Our first date was at his house, I guess. I was sitting in the living room while Fenix got dressed. His mom was curled into a corner of the couch in a pair of purple sweatpants, and I answered her questions the best I could.

"Fenix tells me your dad's a Park Ranger," she tried, and I smiled and nodded. Accurate.

"That must be great. Does your family do a lot of hiking?"

"Not really," I said. Inaccurate. This interview was going terribly.

Then Fenix poked his head in the room, and I was relieved.

"You want a cup of coffee?" he asked his mom.

"No thanks, why?" she asked.

"Just *asking,*" he snapped, disappearing into the hallway again. "I was trying to be *nice.*"

I would have gotten in trouble if I'd talked to my parents that way, but I figured it didn't matter because he was older.

"He probably made coffee for himself and then changed his mind," she rolled her eyes. I shrugged. Maybe.

Finally, he reappeared, in jeans and a green sweater, half-smiling. "Want a tour?" he asked, and for the first time, his mom witnessed my huge smile and said, "Have fun."

Outside, streetlamps illuminated patches of the yellow-green grass, and there wasn't much to see. There were a few trees, and I had the best time walking with him in the chilly night air, holding his hand and hearing the breeze ruffle up the leaves between his commentary.

"There's the shed," he said, and I said, "Wooow," just like my mom did when she was poking fun at my dad.

"Oh, and here's the best part," he said, and I could hear his genuine excitement. He said the next words slowly, and with pride, "The Mustang."

I could just see the outline of a car sitting alone in the dark. It was bulky and angular, and we sat inside it for a few minutes listening to his music until maybe he got bored, waiting for me to make out with him. But I didn't think about that then. I was just following along, having fun. I liked sitting with him in the car. It was a novelty to me—boys with cars—with a license and the promise to take me out.

After that, there was nothing else to see, and as we wandered aimlessly, hand in hand, I wondered if we would take a walk around the neighborhood. I couldn't see what he was getting at, though I remember laughing a lot. There would have been spinning and chasing and rough-and-tumble play, because that's how I flirted—with my whole body, and then he collapsed into the grass, dragging me down with him like we were in a romcom.

He was lying flat on the ground, looking up at me and smiling with questions in his eyes—his face, both illuminated by the streetlamps and cast with deep, dark shadows. He was beautiful, and I kissed him impulsively. Even without tongue, it was messy. My lips smashed against his and splayed out across his face, and he didn't mind. I sat up and looked at him with my hair falling down over my shoulder. I loved his smile, and I was already so, so smitten.

When Fenix met Dad, they shook hands like they were trying to kill each other. Then they each took a step back while I watched, wondering what the Hell they were doing. It was a "man" moment, I realized, by the way they both ignored me. And though it was a surface-level conversation about cars and sports, Dad's voice was deeper than normal. He'd puffed his chest out just for Fenix. In turn, Fenix stood up taller.

When Mom asked me to chop the tomatoes for tacos, I was grateful for the distraction. Over dinner, Dad smiled more easily, asking Fenix about his plans for college, and the night seemed to relax on its own. After three tacos and too many awkward silences, I cleared the plates and grabbed Monopoly.

The game began like it always does, with the buying of rainbow-colored properties and the pain in the ass payments of 14 or 22 dollars. Nothing crazy happened, like it does in some games, where one person gets sent to jail five times in a row, and you get to make up a story about their undercover criminal life. We just collected properties—Mom, Dad, my new boyfriend, and I—at a steady, leisurely pace, until finally, something exciting happened.

Fenix landed on *Chance*. He drew the card from the center of the sea green board and read, "Get a hundred dollars," before lying it face down on the table between us.

"Yay!" I shouted, genuinely excited for him, and as Mom, designated banker by choice, reached for a hundred-dollar bill, I picked up the card to see the picture—and the story. Was it a giant tax refund, or did Fenix win the Nobel Peace Prize? (These things were important.) But my smile slipped. Mr. Monopoly was frowning. "It says pay twenty-five dollars," I blurted out, and I saw, out of the corner of my eye, Mom's head jerk in my direction.

"Oh," Fenix said, shuffling through his money for a twenty and a five. Maybe if we'd been closer, I'd have laughed in his face. But for now, my parents and I smiled secretly at each other. Wrong house. We didn't cheat.

I don't know what I thought dating would be like. Laughter and snuggling. Holding hands. Finding my person.

Fenix and I didn't go out on dates. It was just going over to each other's houses, which wasn't a problem for me. I'd never been in a boy's room before, and I liked the feeling of existing in that space, like I was part of his life.

Upstairs, in a room almost as big as my house, blank white walls met the dark wooden floors of his bedroom. Dusty memories cluttered the top of his dresser—his old dog in a silver frame, a green ribbon from elementary school for perfect attendance. A Little League trophy.

"What position did you play?" I asked.

"What was your dog's name?"

"You never missed a day of school?"

He loved talking about himself, and I loved listening to him talk. I wanted to know everything about him. But after a few weeks, we reached the same point in our relationship as when Christopher had broken up with me. Fenix's room would have gotten exceptionally boring if one of two things didn't happen—either I started making out with him so that there was more to do, or he started grilling me about it so that there was more to contemplate. Each had its own reign.

It started with Fenix sticking his tongue in my mouth and my whole body going rigid with fear.

"Does my breath stink?" he finally asked.

"No."

"Then why won't you kiss me?"

"I am kissing you."

What could I say? I wished that I wanted to kiss him with tongue. I just didn't.

"Why won't you make out with me?" he demanded the next week. "What am I going to do when I introduce you to people—friends we meet together? *This is my girlfriend. We're really in love, see?*" He leaned down to kiss the air, and then he was me, wiggling his tongue and having a seizure.

I sat down on the bed, mentally exhausted, and he sat down next to me. Then I leaned my forehead into his shoulder and took a deep breath, preparing to be vulnerable for possibly the first time in my entire life.

"Listen," I said into his shirt. "I've never made out with anyone before, and I'm scared."

His smile was so big, he didn't even give me time to feel like an idiot. His laugh was tremendous—sexy and deep with relief as he slammed his back into my orange, polka dot comforter. Finally, he stopped asking me about it, and a few weeks later, when it finally happened, it was intuitive.

In the dark, in his bedroom, I lunged my tongue into his mouth in earnest. "You're an amazing kisser," he whispered. "You sure you've never made out with anyone before?"

The day I made out with Fenix, he was happy for five minutes, and then he wanted more. Ezra was right. My life became a series of hurdles—a predestined trajectory of sexual experiences, in very specific order: tongue, hand job, blow job, penetration.

At first I saw clearly, in little comments that he made or the way he positioned his body in front of me. "That was weird," I told him. "You pressured me into doing that." But he had a way of taking my story away from me. And he used my words to craft a narrative that better suited him. I ended up apologizing a lot.

Nobody told me what sex was supposed to be like. I didn't know that condoms kept you safe and in school. So when he said it would feel better for me if we didn't use one, I didn't argue. Instead, I prayed that this was the final step to me becoming a really great girlfriend.

It happened at his house, in his room, with the door closed and his mom downstairs. The buildup was fun. I could have done without the rest of it. I just thought—maybe this is stupid—that losing my virginity was going to be special. But he started off behind my back. I craned my neck to see him. I wanted to tell him that I loved him, but my voice faded into a question.

"What?" he said. "Oh. I love you too."

I got the feeling he wished I would shut up.

At the end of the day, sex hurt. I felt claustrophobic and disappointed, and on top of everything, he wanted to keep it a secret between the two of us.

"That's what mature couples do," he told me. He also said that this was the best things got for me, since women couldn't actually orgasm—and bless my heart, I believed him.

It slipped when Alex was talking shit about all the people she knew who didn't wear condoms. She was curled into the giant red loveseat, counting them all on her fingers. "Annie's boyfriend doesn't wear a condom. Shannon. Breanna. Charlie! And she's smart, too."

I was pouring myself a bowl of Cinnamon Toast Crunch.

"How stupid can you be?"

"Is it that big of a deal?" I asked, grabbing the milk from the fridge. "Me and Fenix don't use condoms." But her face. I realized immediately. Like I'd punched her in the gut.

"I'm sorry," I said. She had texted me within minutes of losing her virginity. "Hey, I'm sorry," I tried again, crumbling, seeing those sad shoulders.

"Fenix didn't want me to tell anyone."

She told me everything. We'd sat on her bed until four in the morning while she answered every sex question I'd always been too afraid to ask. She'd been so excited then. This wasn't how it was supposed to be.

Her green eyes filled with tears. "Please don't get pregnant," her voice cracked.

"I won't," I begged. "I won't, Alex." Just please don't be mad at me.

"That's so unsafe. Please—please don't get pregnant."

"I won't. I promise you. I'm not going to."

But I didn't know if she was crying because I'd betrayed her or if she was genuinely worried. Yes, I was reckless. Sure, every time I had sex without a condom, I was putting myself at risk of pregnancy or STDs. I knew that, somewhere in my brain.

But the moment felt bigger, somehow. Alex was catching onto something.

"This is a real relationship," Fenix liked to say, "where we talk about things." But talking always led to arguments, and in person, all he wanted to do was have sex.

On the phone, he picked fights, but I wasn't worried about it because I thought I could hold my own. That, or my love would be strong enough to change him into someone who was nicer to me. But as it turned out, I couldn't do anything right. And I had way more flaws than I thought.

When I wore fuzzy boots with checkered pants, he said I had no fashion sense.

When I liked a song but didn't know the band, he said I was a poser.

When I got straight A's, he asked me why I acted so stupid.

When I made him a grilled cheese sandwich, he said his grandma's was better.

When I posted a picture on Social, he said I looked like a slut.

When I cried, I was being too sensitive, and when I laughed, I was being immature.

"What will your boss think when you get a job?" he asked. "You have to have tools in your toolbox, Chloe. You have to be mature."

I was passing my mom in the hallway then, as I shouted, "You're not my BOSS!"

She laughed, and it would have been a funny thing for me to say if it had been in response to literally anything else. But I was being for real. He wasn't my boss.

I escaped to Florida with Alex and her parents. For spring break, they rented a beach apartment in St. Pete, and Fenix wanted to talk on the phone in the morning, at night, and in the middle of the day. I tried to be discreet about it, but Alex's mom rolled her eyes.

"She has to go call her *boyfriend*," she snickered, as I opened the sliding glass door to the balcony. But as soon as the door was wide enough to flee, a tornadolike gust of wind rushed past me, picking up the cream-colored blackout curtains and violently thrashing them around the living room.

Wide-eyed and frozen, I watched in horror as they knocked over a lamp, shattering the bulb and continuing their fury, as Elaine screamed, "SHUT THE DOOR! SHUT THE DOOR!"

Finally, I jumped out onto the balcony and slammed the door closed as fast as I could. My heart pounded as I stared at my hands, still clenched around the wooden door handle. Inside, the curtains settled, and I caught my breath before cautiously easing my way back inside.

Elaine was slumped over in a chair, looking despondently into her hands at two broken pieces of a perfect conch shell.

"I'm so sorry," I said, my voice childish with anxiety. "I don't know what happened."

"When you opened the door to the balcony," she said, "Paul was coming in through the front door, and you created a wind tunnel."

From then on, I always checked that the navy door on the opposite end of the house was closed when I called Fenix.

Between phone calls, Alex and I swam in the ocean and laid out on the beach every day. We went on a sail boating excursion, and it gave me life. I loved the way the boat smashed into the deep blue water, and the wind whipped my ponytail until all my curls were tangled. I laughed out of pure happiness, and Alex and I swore that we'd learn to sail together one day.

For lunch, we ate outside under a blue and white umbrella, and Alex and I ordered virgin strawberry daiquiris. I was relaxed, for once, sitting in the shade with my friend and those I had come to think of as my family, when I started feeling nauseous and excused myself. Through a maze of tables and into the air-conditioned restaurant, the bathroom was empty. In the stall, I knelt beside the toilet, reading the notes scrawled onto the walls, wondering if I would throw up.

You are beautiful.

Jennifer's a slut.

But nothing happened.

Eventually I stood up and washed my hands in the sink. Then on my way out of the bathroom, I caught my reflection in a wide, full-length mirror, and stopped. Like I was seeing myself for the first time. I was drawn in by this person, and I walked up to the mirror until my nose was nearly touching the glass.

Who's in there? I wanted to know, looking deeply into my hazel, gold-flecked eyes. It was the first time I ever wondered about myself. What was happening with me? Where was I? But eventually, I had to walk back to the table, where my coconut shrimp was waiting for me.

"How's your boyfriend?" Alex's mom smirked when I was back at the table. I pulled my phone out of my purse, which had been hanging over the side of the chair, and I showed it to her.

"I don't know."

Back home, my role in the relationship became a blank space that occasionally reached out to validate him. Over the phone, Fenix talked about sushi one night for hours, the eye of the storm between gnarly bouts of insults. Lying in bed, I tried to maintain a silent, genuine interest, and forget about when he said I wasn't as pretty as I thought. Sushi. *I've never even had sushi,* I thought, my tired eyes resting on the lava lamp.

Two blue globs oozed into one another when Mom poked her head in the door.

"Can we talk?" she asked, forcing herself to smile.

"We should run away together," Fenix was saying. "We can live in an apartment in the city and have sex whenever we want."

"Hold on, Fenix," I interrupted. "My mom wants to talk to me."

"About what?"

"I don't know."

With reluctance, I put his voice down on the bed and walked into the hallway. Mom closed the door and stood in front of me. I was trapped.

"You have to promise not to tell Fenix, okay?" Her voice was small and hoarse, like she was trying not to cry.

"What is it, Mom?" My heart ached.

"You have to promise."

"I won't, what is it?"

"I'm so worried about you," she said, her eyes wide.

I hated this.

Her hair was pulled back in a ponytail, her bangs shoved under a black headband, as she looked up at me, pleading. "I don't know what to do, as your mom. I feel like he's *hurting* you, Chloe." Tears slipped down her face.

"I don't know what to do," she said, covering her face as she choked on the tears.

"No, Mama," I whispered in her ear, feeling the warmth of her sadness. "I'm okay." But everything was all wrong. "I promise you. I'm okay. I love you."

"Okay," she said, sniffing back her tears. "Alright. I just want to make sure you're okay."

"Love you, Mom." I kissed her cheek.

"I love you too, Chloe."

Then I closed the door on her and went back to my place on the bed, against the wall with my knees to my chest.

"Hey," I sighed into the phone, relieved to be away from the sadness.

But the first thing he said was, "What did your mom say?"

Then he pried it out of me like tree roots from the earth, and I felt sad and evil and dead.

I told Fenix my biggest secret because I wanted him to know me.

Before Fenix, there was this girl, an exchange student from Spain with bright eyes and long red hair. It spilled down her back and over her chair in Algebra, two seats up and one row to the left. She was so pretty, with her perfect teeth and crooked nose.

I thought that was it. I could appreciate a pretty girl. But I caught myself staring at her. And it wasn't just her face I was looking at. It was her clothes. The way they clung to her body. The way she moved underneath them. I wondered what she would look like without them—fuck! Then I pushed those thoughts away until the day she wore a pair of light, faded jeans with a gaping hole over her thigh, and I finally understood the no holes in jeans policy.

As the teacher carried on in his dull, monotone voice, I bored my eyes into the desk, heat rising steadily into my cheeks. There was no getting around it anymore. Not only was I bi, I wanted to be with Isla in a way that I'd never wanted to be with a boy.

When I told Ezra, he'd screamed with happiness.

"YAY! Another rainbow child in Blue Rock!" And he gave me confidence—that I wasn't crazy or imagining things. That I could kiss a boy and like a girl, and there was nothing innately confusing about that. I just liked who I liked.

Obviously, I wasn't expecting the same reaction from Fenix. I just hoped that if I told him something he didn't already know about me, he would see me more clearly. As a dynamic human with passion and layers. Worthy of empathy. Interesting. At the very least, I figured he would think it was hot.

"You want to know a secret?"

I'd been walking circles around my bedroom, working up the nerve to tell him.

"A secret?" Finally, I heard his smile through the phone. "Yeah."

It had been weeks since he'd been interested in anything I had to say.

"Well—not that you have to worry or anything," I prefaced, "but—before we met—I totally had a crush on Isla."

In the millisecond before he spoke, a weight lifted off my shoulders that I didn't know existed. One more person knew the real me.

But all he said was, "Oh. Doesn't everyone?"

And he reminded me that there was no real me. That I wasn't interesting or hot or passionate or layered, and that I was just like everybody else.

When he flirted with her in front of me, jealousy mixed with bile in my throat.

"Her boyfriend says that in bed, Isla does really sexy, exotic Spanish shit. What can you do?" he whispered in my ear.

I laughed, pretending he'd made a joke. But I didn't know whether he was trying to insult me, make me jealous, or turn me on.

Then he frowned. "Not that much, huh?"

He was testing my limits, and apparently, I didn't have any. Fenix called my parents stupid, accused my future self of

cheating on him because he could tell I was a "whore by na-
ture," and then he tried to get me to say that I would marry
him, all in the same day. He was starting to scare me. I had
given him everything—my brain, my soul, my body—and it
wasn't enough. There were no more milestones. Nothing happened after penetration. He wasn't my true love. He was a
fucking psycho.

I was reading *The Hunger Games*. Mom was folding laundry beside me on the couch. The clothes were warm on my feet when Dad walked through the door.

"Hey!" he said, taking off his work boots and kissing Mom on the lips. Then he stood facing us, pressing the tips of his fingers together, until Mom said, "What happened?"

They knew each other so well.

"There's a job opening up in Virginia Beach."

I jolted upright, losing my place in the book.

"YES!" I said, heartbeat pounding in my chest. He stood, stuck with his mouth hanging open while I looked at him with a certainty I hadn't felt in months.

"Dad, yes. *Apply.*" While my parents looked at each other—full wordless sentences they thought I couldn't read.

"Don't you want to think about it?" he asked.

"No. I'm positive." I couldn't think about Ezra or Alex. There was only Fenix and my ticket out.

We set a date for the Tripod meeting, but there was nothing to talk about. Sitting on the floor with our feet in a triangle, their worried eyes bored into me, prickling my skin until I looked away. "I want to move. What else do you want me to say?"

I spoke from under the weight of extreme exhaustion. But in my mind, I was laughing. I was back on the beach. Alex and I were learning to sail.

When Dad got the job, I wasn't shocked or excited, because I'd already known in my heart that we were going. It wasn't an adventure. It was a need. It was movement—the migration of butterflies.

"It'll be fun," I told Ezra, my words breathy and non-convincing. "You can visit me at the beach."

"Yeah," he said softly. "It'll be fun."

But he didn't talk for the rest of the day, and I didn't notice.

What's weird is that, even though I wanted to move, I still didn't want to break up with Fenix because I didn't know it was possible to break up with someone you loved. I needed help.

I told my History teacher, Mrs. Johnson, because she was an adult, and adults were supposed to know what to do. She was matter-of-fact and grandmotherly, with long braids from the left side of her head hanging down her right shoulder. "Can we talk?" I asked her after class.

When she sat down at the desk beside me, I started sobbing into my hands.

"I have to tell you something," I heaved. "But you have to promise not to tell."

"I can't promise that," she said, but I kept going. I had to get it out.

"Me and Fenix—he's so mean to me. And we had *sex!*"

That's not what I meant. But how could I explain the torture of being in an emotionally abusive relationship, if I didn't even know I was in one?

Mrs. Johnson paused, touching her fingers to the gold cross around her neck. "Some people can be really sensitive to that," she nodded. "Me—I wouldn't know." Turns out, Mrs. Johnson was a virgin.

"I'll be right back," she said, returning with the English teacher.

Mrs. Shaw had short blue hair and a nose ring. Together, with Mrs. Johnson in the chair and Mrs. Shaw sitting on top of a desk, they listed coping skills I could use once I broke up with Fenix.

Mrs. Shaw: Exercise helps me a lot when I'm feeling down.
Mrs. Johnson: Or eating a giant chocolate bar.
Mrs. Shaw: Oh! Or sometimes, just like sitting in the shower for a couple hours, letting the water wash over you.

I imagined Mrs. Shaw naked in the shower, and I wondered if she'd ever been in this much pain.

Mrs. Johnson: Yeah, that's a good one.
Mrs. Shaw: You should get outside, or—honestly, I like getting sucked into a really trashy romance novel.
Mrs. Johnson: You need to talk to your mom.

That night, Mom and I sat facing each other, cross-legged on my bed, and I told her in the same screechy, horrified voice. "*We had sex!*" Then I bawled my eyes out as she put her arms around me and cried too.

But the moment was short-lived. The second I wiped away the last of my tears, my emotions fell away. My brain remelted.

"His penis is so big," I said. Then I showed her how long with my fingers, and she said nothing—bewilderment beneath her magnificent brown eyes.

In my mind, telling an adult should have solved everything. In reality, I broke up with Fenix. He cried into the phone, and I changed my mind.

At school the next day, Ezra would barely talk to me, but he just said he was tired, and I was oblivious.

I broke up with Fenix for the last time two weeks before summer break.

Then, when he asked to see me again, I said yes. Of course, I would see him one last time. Closure, right? It was the nice thing to do. But an hour before he was supposed to pick me up, I found myself crying on the porch with my head in my hands. Murky pools of mascara dripped down my nose. *Plop.* Onto the stairs. The sun beat down on my neck as the front door opened behind me. *Plop.* My tears seeped into the wood.

I barely looked up to see Dad, stopping halfway out the front door, like he already knew he wasn't invited. Then he sat down beside me on the stairs anyway and asked, "What's wrong, Clo?"

I thought about it for a minute, and with a canyon-sized ache in my heart, I said, "Fenix tricked me. I'm in love with someone who doesn't exist."

Dad put his arm around my shoulders and squeezed my tiny, dejected body while I cried. Then he leaned his head down so he could see my eyes, and he asked, "Instead of hanging out with Fenix tonight, would you want to go out for ice cream—with me?"

I smiled then, realizing that it was all I'd ever wanted in a relationship. Ice cream. Love.

And in between sniffles, I said, "Yeah. That sounds really good."

We went inside together, and I called Fenix in the living room in front of my parents.

"Hey," I said, smiling into the phone. "I'm not coming tonight. I'm going out with my dad for ice cream instead."

"Really?" he said. It was his favorite word to use against me. "Are you serious, Chloe?" Like I was making the worst decision of my life—like I was the stupidest person on Earth.

I could feel my parents' eyes on me, wondering what I was going to do, as I said, "Yeah, really."

Whatever words he shouted over the line sounded silly, and I giggled as I hung up on him in the middle of his sentence.

Then I looked at my parents with a big goofy smile, and my mom put her hand up for a high five. "Way to go, girl," she said. The spell was broken.

Though I wasn't perfect. Even after a cotton candy ice cream cone with Oreos and gummy bears, Fenix tricked me one last time.

Seniors didn't have to come to school for the last week, and knowing that we would never see each other again made everything easier. But he messaged me, asking if I wanted to see him Wednesday. He would come, he said, just to see me one last time.

My heart melted. Despite everything, I did miss him, and I took his message as a sign that perhaps our love had been real after all, even if we weren't meant to be together.

Wednesday morning, I went to school nervous with anticipation. Where would he be? How would he find me? I expected him around every corner. But as the day went on, as I looked for him in all our old meeting spots, my excitement turned to dread. He wasn't there. *But he wouldn't do that to me,* I told myself, even as the final bell rang. He was probably waiting for me in the bus loop.

Standing alone by the red brick wall, I looked around with my phone clutched in my hand, expecting him to text me, any moment now. But there was no text. No one came traipsing up to meet me. No one scooped me up for one last hug. He didn't come.

He just wanted to make me cry one last time.

For Ezra's seventeenth birthday, we threw a surprise party at the cabin with a dinosaur cake and a scavenger hunt.

"Everybody partner up!" Mom instructed.

I felt a jolt of anxiety in my chest as I avoided eye contact with my friends. While I didn't want to look desperate, I didn't want to be partners with anyone except Ezra. But he immediately skipped over to me, like it was the easiest decision in the world.

"I don't know what we're doing," he said, "but we're gonna kill 'em." Confidence renewed, I pointed finger guns at the opposing teams—Nicolas and Malik, Olivia and Alex.

"Stupify!" Malik shouted, pointing a stick at Ezra, and as Mom passed out her handwritten scavenger hunt lists, Ezra mumbled something about guns versus wands.

"Alright, everyone!" Mom yelled over the chaos. "There's no time limit. Whichever team finds everything on the list first, wins." In a rush of adrenaline, Ezra and I scanned the list.

A picture of your partner doing a handstand against a tree.

"On your marks!" Mom shouted.

A rock bigger than your fist.

"Get set!"

A live insect.

"GO!"

And we scattered.

"Come on!" Ezra shouted, crossing the gravel road and sprinting towards a tree. I ran after him, the scavenger hunt list flapping wildly in my hand. Then he got down on his knees as I pulled out my phone. He walked his feet backwards up the trunk, and I snapped the picture like my life depended on it.

"Got it!" I said, scrambling for a rock as he flopped down to his feet.

We dashed around the cabin, sweating through our shirts and looking for bugs, high on competition until we'd found everything on the list except for something red. But even splitting up to increase our chances of finding anything, not a red leaf, or a bottlecap, or a caterpillar with a red stripe appeared.

I ran up and down the gravel loop, searching the grass on one side and then the other, watching the other teams in horror as they continued to mark things off their lists, when I heard Ezra yell, "Chloe, I GOT IT!"

My shoes tore through the grass as I raced towards him. He stood still, fiddling with the blue birthday pin Mom had given him. Then he pulled it off his shirt and stabbed himself in the finger, squeezing out a drop of blood that made me laugh and shriek with joy.

"IT'S RED!!!" I screamed. "Ezra, YOU'RE A GENIUS!!!!" Then we sprinted back to the cabin, and that's how we won—my mom, equally impressed and concerned.

While my parents finished packing, I was trapped with Alex at her grandma's lakehouse. It was one of those beautiful days where the sun was hot, and the wind was cool, and I hated Alex with my whole body. I was sitting alone in the gazebo by the water, not knowing what to do with the rage flooding through my bloodstream. I couldn't stand to be around her.

I hoped I was embarrassing her. I hoped her family asked her where I was, and she couldn't think of anything to say. We'd been fighting all day.

The night before, I was in the top bunk, half-reading, half-talking. Alex was sitting in front of the mirror, wiping her face with makeup remover, when I decided to tell her the secret I'd been holding in forever. What could it hurt? I was leaving, anyway.

"What is it?" she smiled.

And the words left my body in a flood of relief—just to hear them in the air. "I really, really, really like Ezra," I said, hiding my face in my book.

"Well, yeah," she rolled her eyes. "That's obvious."

"Really?" I asked, trying to match her composure. This wasn't what I was expecting.

"Yeah. He likes you too."

"What?" I asked, as she rummaged through her suitcase. "No, he doesn't. *How?"* Ezra was gay. He didn't like me. He couldn't.

"Because he *told me*," she snapped.

If Ezra liked me back, then why was she getting annoyed? Why wouldn't she want her two best friends to be happy together?

"He loves you," she said flatly.

"How do you know?" I asked, still not believing her—yet desperately wanting to.

"Because he said, *I love her.*"

For a moment, a beam of light burst through my soul. I felt the miracle and the possibility and the crushing reality of my leaving, when she looked me dead in the eyes.

"And just to let you know, I wouldn't be friends with you anymore if you were together."

"Why?" All my dreams shriveled up in my chest.

"Because I'd be a third wheel."

On moving day, Alex and I played cards on the floor of my empty bedroom. Cross-legged in our pajamas, we smiled too much and forced our laughter—one last memory before I left, and I couldn't even cry. When she hugged me in the doorway, my heart throbbed with the intricate sadness of letting go— of saying goodbye and knowing that our friendship was over. *I love you, I love you, I love you.* We said it a million times, and I think we meant it.

But I hadn't made plans with her like I had with Ezra. He was coming to Virginia Beach next month. *Soon,* I told myself, whenever I saw his face in my head. His wide smile. His brown eyes. And that's as far as I would let myself think. He would come to the beach, and I would go to Blue Rock, and we would be best friends forever, as long as we lived, because there could be no other way.

I wondered about the others—Malik, Nicolas, and Olivia.

"I'll come back," I promised. "We'll never stop being friends."

I pretended that it was no big deal—that I was so confident.

"It's just a few hours," I said, as if time and distance meant nothing.

But the thought of forgetting about them—my friends, who gave me life—terrified me. First, I'd forget their favorite colors. Then their birthdays. The sound of their laughing. Even worse, maybe one day, I wouldn't even care.

"I have something for you," Malik said, the last time I saw him. It was a tiny cardboard jewelry box labeled, *The Rookery* in pretty gold letters. We were sitting on the bed of the kids' room, just the two of us, and all I could think about while he watched me open it was my reaction. Whatever it was, would I be sad, grateful, or happy enough? And would my feelings be reflected on my face, as he watched me with those soft, eager eyes? I didn't want to hurt him—sweet Malik. But when I opened the box, it didn't matter what I looked like.

He'd written a note in black ink on lined yellow paper and folded it a thousand times into a small square. *Enclosed is a friendship bracelet (I have one too so we will always be friends) and a dollar to get you through the tough times and a seashell.*

He tied the orange string bracelet around my wrist, and all at once, I was sad, grateful, and honored. His gift was all and everything he could have given me, and it was everything I needed, including a promise that we wouldn't forget each other. Really truly, he believed that we would be friends forever. So, I did, too.

With arms like bricks, I loaded boxes into the moving truck under an abrasive August sun. My eyes burned from crying. My heart was achy and broken as I walked through the cabin for the last time. It was no longer ours. My life in Blue Rock was over, and I hoped to God that I hadn't made a mistake.

Our first night in Virginia Beach was Mom's birthday. Dad walked down with us to the northern beaches, the water of the Chesapeake Bay slipping dark and silently under the long bridge linking my new home to the Delmarva Peninsula, our flip-flops slapping against the pavement of the empty park roads. Crickets chirped along the edges of the grass, and we were weary and happy. From our new house, the bay was only half a mile away, across the silent nighttime highway.

Through the long, carless parking lot, we walked towards the water, the shushing of the waves growing louder with every step. Tall reeds shifted like shadows, and the night felt pivotal and mysterious. As we reached the shoreline, I kicked off my shoes, and I could just make out the darkness of the Chesapeake Bay. With the cold sand under our feet, Mom and I ran towards the water and cheered.

"Happy birthday, Mom!" I shouted over the noisy, ambling waves. She wore a navy-blue swimsuit with a halter top and a skirt that covered up the parts of her legs that she hated. She was jumping up and down, her feet barely coming off the ground as she waved her chunky arms, chanting, "Virginia Beach! Virginia Beach!"

The bay dealt black boiling waves with gray crests and a hushing melody as we shouted, "It's going to be the best year EVER!" Still, the bay—northern lovechild of the ocean and the Eastern Shore, was humbling to our riot. We could fill up a house with our laughter, but the beach was so much bigger—haunting almost in the way it drowned out even our greatest hopes and happiness. Dad chuckled lightly and raised a fist to the best year ever, and I truly believed it would be.

Then Mom stepped into a giant hole, invisible in the darkness, and fell back onto her bottom with a thump.

"Humph!" she frowned, and we all laughed.

Dad and I sat down around the edges of the hollow beside her, our feet going in towards the center like the spokes of a wheel, just being together, as a Tripod, until we realized that we were sitting in a giant mosquitos' nest that eventually sent us back home.

Our new home. Together. Fenix behind me, the future in front. My mom, my dad and me. Our Tripod. Inseparable.

PART II

Age 19

Two years after my parents' divorce, Dad picked me up from college. At Waffle House, we drank cheap, hot coffee while the snow flurried out the window, and I went on and on about my new life, as if winter break wouldn't be enough time to tell him everything.

Soft, half-eaten waffles crowded the sticky two-seater booth between us, when he finally asked, "Did you get my letter?"

"A letter?" I smiled. "What was it?"

Like a little kid, I still loved getting mail.

"*Shit.*" He leaned back into the booth, looking behind him. "I thought you were just avoiding it."

"Avoiding what?" I asked, the air thick like the syrup on my plate.

"I have a new roommate," he mumbled.

I looked at him without speaking. I didn't know what he meant.

"Mary," he said, and I understood.

It was her. The other woman.

"It's just temporary," he said. "I really wanted you to have a heads up."

"Yeah," I breathed, reorganizing my brain. Just a year before, I'd messaged her over Social and told her to leave us the fuck alone. I promised myself that if I ever saw her, I would beat her into oblivion, and then I threatened to key her car if

I ever saw it in the neighborhood. All of these thoughts meshed together in my brain, and now here she was.

"I'm curious to meet her," I told him. It was the closest version of the truth.

"Really?" Disbelief danced in his eyes, and he almost smiled. I guessed this was going better than he'd expected.

"Yeah." All I knew was that she liked bird watching and riding bikes, and Mom didn't. There must have been something so amazing about her—something better than me and Mom combined. "She's like a shadow."

When he called to tell her the news, I heard her voice for the first time through the phone. "This is a miracle!" she shouted, so happy she was laughing, and I thought that maybe we had a chance at becoming friends.

I don't remember meeting Mary for the first time, but I remember Christmas morning. Dad gave me a pair of binoculars and a field guide to birds of North America, and the three of us stopped at a gas station for hot black coffee. Mary wore a green puffy coat, her head down against the wind as she wrapped her arms around her tiny, 26-year-old body.

A black crow on a power line clashed against the white sky, and I flipped through the pages of my new book. *American Crow.*

"What should I write?" I asked Dad, breathing clouds into the freezing winter.

"Just the date and where you saw the bird."

"A power line?"

"Wawa on Shore Drive," he said. And so, it began.

If there was a bird in a tree, Dad pointed with frantic enthusiasm. "Chloe, Chloe!" He didn't want me to miss the tufted titmouse in the parking lot.

He liked waterfowl best and drove me and Mary around town to the best places to find them. In a pond full of garbage behind the library, there was a cormorant and a mallard duck with a green, emerald neck. In a ditch like a stream at the end of Pleasure House Road, I recorded seeing a great blue heron and a hooded merganser. Then we stopped on the Lesner Bridge and saw a different kind of merganser floating in the Chesapeake Bay. Mostly, I looked at the birds through my binoculars while Mary and Dad discussed the species. Then, when they decided what kind of bird it was, I wrote it down.

Did Mary speak besides that? I have no idea. My memories of her are recorded as blank space. I sat behind her in the car so it would be easier to talk to Dad, and I can see the side of the back of her head in the passenger's seat—flat, brown, shoulder-length hair. I hear her voice like a sarcastic, high-pitched country song, but nothing sticks.

That night, Dad and I visited Mom's new place. She'd put all the old furniture in storage and was renting a room now from a nice enough, monotone Jewish woman named Sara. Sara sprawled out on the couch with a bored expression on her face, and she watched while the three of us sat on the white, sterile carpet, opening presents from under the stunning blue and silver Hanukkah tree. Eventually, Sara yawned, retreating to her bedroom for a nap. When we finished Christmas and there was nothing left to say, we put our feet together to make a triangle—the Tripod.

Dad's head dropped, his shoulders quaking. Tears streamed down his beet red face.

"I'm sorry for ruining this family," he choked. An iridescent bubble formed and popped on his lips. Mom and I held his hands. *Of course, he didn't. Of course, we'd always be a family.*

These are the words we said, and they felt true at the time. But that was the last Tripod.

At Dad's house—our old house—I smiled at Mary over dinner and asked her when she was leaving. He'd said it was temporary. But I realized that was a lie when her blue eyes went wide, and she looked down at the table before answering.

"I'm not exactly sure," she said softly.

Dad told me later that she cried. "That really hurt her feelings," he said, and as my heart coiled inside my chest, I didn't know what to say. It was meant to.

If I liked her at all, I couldn't. I hated her, but I couldn't, and I felt guilty in every direction. When I left to go back to school, I said bye and nothing else. What could I say? She was my family's homewrecker, and everything at home felt wrecked.

But it wasn't a shock. Not really. In hindsight, it was as clear as her wide blue eyes.

Age 17

Junior year of high school, Dad bought the two of us front-row tickets to the circus, and it was everything I needed—an arena so bright and magnificent, booming with sounds and colors—air like glitter. There was no room for melancholy.

A young, purple-haired twenty-something winked at me before sprinting onto the floor, backflipping into center stage. Beautiful people in silver, sparkling leotards rode wrinkled elephants. Flying trapeze artists soared through the air, and my heart soared with them.

At intermission, Dad and I shared a giant bag of popcorn, and then it was time for Dad's favorite act, the Globe of Death. When I was little, I used to hold my breath, waiting for the motorcycles to crash in the cage. Now I knew that there was nothing to fear except my own beating heart.

The end brought confetti, a light show, and happiness for days.

"You really think I could be in the circus?" Dad asked me that night, wide-eyed and smiling.

We were sharing a booth in a dim, orange-hued restaurant, as Mom stared at us across the table, gritting her teeth.

"You should apply to clown school!" I laughed. "Actually, I have to start thinking about college soon. Maybe I should apply to clown school."

"What do you think, Amber?"

"Where will we *live?*" Mom asked, her tone cold.

I rolled my eyes. "Don't be such a party pooper."

Together, Dad and I fantasized about a circus train, like in *Water for Elephants*—or maybe a caravan these days. There'd be parties every night. I'd flirt with all the cute, purple-haired clowns, traveling and manifesting the fullest expression of myself—wild and free. And Dad—he'd be a great clown. I imagined him waving to all the boys and girls in the crowd before his debut juggling act. Mom and I in the audience cheering—laughing—jumping up and down even.

What couldn't she see?

Beside a cheery yellow wall, Mom and I painted pottery in the back corner of a local studio. She had a half-finished vase in front of her and a thick bristled brush with pastel paint in her hand. I had a blank plate and no plan, but eventually, a grey aspen forest began to emerge—vertical lines with stripes and eyes. Then, as I paused to consider my next move, Mom started telling me some strange story about Dad wanting to be like Chris McCandless from *Into the Wild*.

"If he leaves to roam the Earth or something," the pink rims of her eyes began to swell, "we're going to be just fine, okay?"

"What?" my head jerked. Right in public, she was starting to cry.

"Mom," I said. "Dad's not going anywhere. I promise."

What was she talking about?

"It's okay, Mom," I said, speaking to her as if she were a child. Was she going crazy? Was this the onset of dementia?

"You're right," she sniffled, quickly wiping a tear from her cheek. "Daddy's not going anywhere."

And that was it. It was settled.

In the aspen forest, a girl emerged on my plate, naked and alone, with orange nipples and creamy pink skin. A massive green shadow lurked menacingly between the trees, and I didn't know why.

Dad's eyes were blue, but they lost their color that year. He started skipping the fifteen-year tradition of tucking Mom in every night. He didn't care if the covers were just right. She went to bed without a kiss, and he slept on the couch.

No one talked about the rising tension—the growing silence between the three of us. What was there to say? He was only sleeping. But I watched him one night, sprawl out onto the creamy yellow couch and fluff the pillow behind his head. I saw how relaxed he looked as he pulled out his phone, and for the first time, I felt the ice-cold rage that had been crawling under my skin.

"Well, don't you look comfortable," I spat, ready to fight, but he just smirked like a stupid teenager.

"Yep."

Then he looked back at his phone, and I swear to God, I could barely see as I walked into my parents' bedroom and grabbed the books off his bedside table.

I walked outside, catching thorns in my bare feet, and I chucked them into the fire pit: *Everett Ruess: A Vagabond for Beauty, Into Thin Air,* and especially *Into the Wild.*

I poured lighter fluid on those books that I loved, that made me love my dad even more. Then I set them on fire and watched them burn while I waited for him to stop me, to come running outside and tell me I was grounded or ask me what was wrong or call me disrespectful, so I could say,

"FUCK YOU, YOU PIECE OF SHIT, I THOUGHT YOU LOVED US."

But he never came, and he never asked. And he never read those books again because they were already lodged in his heart.

Later that night, Dad finally went to bed with Mom, sleeping late into the morning. I was reading on the loveseat. In the background of my story, the blow dryer roared and stopped in the bathroom. I imagined Mom reaching for her makeup bag and plugging in the straightener. Their bedroom door clicked open and shut, as quietly as she could. As I sank deeper into my book, she was trying not to wake him.

Thundering footsteps brought me back into the house. The door burst open as Mom stormed out of the bedroom and into the kitchen. There was a crash. Dad shouted her name. "Amber!" Then he chased her out the door.

I rushed into the kitchen. The family photo albums were splayed out onto the black and white tile—the crash. I stepped over them to see out the window. This was the pinnacle—the moment of truth, and I needed to know.

In the yard, Dad wore a gray shirt and gym shorts. He stood barefoot with his hands on his hips, and he wouldn't look at her. Mom scrolled through his phone in the speckled, early morning sun. She was ready for work, in black slacks and a polka dot blouse, thin and loose around her body, as I held my breath, seeing everything—Mom's wrinkles; Dad's eyes; her hips tilted, as drastically as the world on its axis.

But nothing happened. She handed him his phone and walked back towards the house.

"Sleeping with your phone under your pillow," Mom jeered as they walked through the door. *"Yeah, right."*

Then she left for work. He disappeared, and there was only silence.

I stormed into my parents' bedroom, shaking with fury. Dad's change jar was sitting on the dresser—six inches wide and a foot and a half tall, with a metal lid that latched. It was full and heavy, and I took the whole thing.

At the grocery store, I poured years of Dad's extra change into the green coin machine. Then I focused on the clatter of the coins falling down into the vat, the rising number on the screen—*don't think, don't think, don't think.* Until finally, I had over a hundred bucks.

Nearly blind with my trembling heart, I managed to find the floral department and fill my cart with apologies. Red tulips first, before a bundle of sunflowers—like Mom's smile. This was justice. Vibrant pink carnations. Peach roses because she deserved them. Orange lilies because she deserved everything, and someone had to give it to her.

In line, standing still, I finally cried. Silent, heavy tears fell from my nose and chin as I paid the cashier, and I thought of telling her that someone had died. It was us. The Tripod was dead.

When my English teacher asked to talk with me after class, I was prepared for the worst—but not this. Sitting across from me, Ms. Hall sat backwards in the blue plastic chair with her elbows folded across the top. Her long flowing skirt draped over her tan legs as she looked towards the ceiling, contemplating her words. I was in trouble. That was obvious. And that was something I could handle. Whatever it was, I already didn't care.

If this meeting was about my eight missing English assignments, Ms. Hall was wasting her time. My brain was stuck in a deep fog. I was numb all over. Nothing could touch me. Then she looked at me, and she said, "You seem, when you're in my class, like you're not really here," and I felt the sadness in my chest like a bullet.

"Is everything okay at home?" she asked gently, and my eyes welled up with tears.

Home.

I didn't think anyone had noticed me.

Home was Dad, sleeping on the couch or not at all—walking barefoot outside in the middle of the night, his dead eyes.

I want to feel the ground on my feet, he said. *I want to know what it means to be alive.*

But did he love us?

"Yeah," I nodded. "Everything's fine."

Home was Mom, asking Dad the same question five times until I finally yelled, "Dad! Mom's talking to you," and him looking up, distracted— "What?"

I felt my cheeks flush red as I swallowed the sobs seconds away from surfacing. But I couldn't. I couldn't feel this right now—not at school.

There were five of us at the reject table. We sat alone—together—in the corner of the roaring cafeteria. Me. The emo girl. The anime kid. The one who ate three cheeseburgers for lunch every day. And Savannah. No one talked much, but Savannah talked to everyone and asked enough questions to get to know people.

The reject table was the closest thing I had to a friend group in Virginia Beach, and Savannah was the closest thing I had to a friend. She didn't mind my thick black eyeliner—which was how I felt—or my glittery eyeshadow—which was how I wanted to feel. And when I felt like an alien version of myself, she made me feel human again.

The Secret Game was her idea.

Now, I wonder if it was all part of the plan. If she just wanted to know my secrets. Or maybe, she really did feel what I felt—the impulsive, cathartic rush of exposing your true self to a group of strangers. The desire to be known.

We cut strips of paper and passed them around the table. The rules of the Secret Game were simple. Everyone wrote down a secret, folded the paper into a tiny square, and put it in the middle of the table. Then, we took turns reading the secrets out loud.

I wrote down a secret that was easy to part with. It was a secret, but I wasn't ashamed of it. It didn't haunt me. I never tried to hide it. It just never seemed to come up—ever.

I like girls.

The most interesting part of the game was after the secret was read aloud, and everyone paused, looking around the table at each person—*who could it be?*—before guessing who wrote it. But no one guessed me. Everyone thought the secret came from a straight boy playing it safe. How wrong they were in assuming that any of us would play it safe.

Sometimes, I want to beat up random people in the street so I can get my anger out.

The boy who drew anime—with his soft eyes and timid jawline—lifted his fingers from the table. *Mine.*

Then he drew a secret.

I'm failing three of my classes.

The girl in the fishnets and black hoodie shrugged.

Last Friday, I made out with my best friend Jeremy in the back of the car.

Followed by manic laughter from the one who ate three cheeseburgers every day.

And finally, Savannah's secret: *I'm bi-curious.*

On the last day of school, she passed me a note.

"Don't read it," she said. "Wait until you get home."

But I couldn't wait.

"I have to pee."

"You're going to read it, aren't you?"

"Maybe," I smiled back at her, already walking away.

In the bathroom stall, with my back against the door, I opened the note. Using a blunt pencil, she'd written in a square like she had her own ideas of where the margins should be.

I'm not bi, but I've been having weird feelings about you.

Weird feelings? Was that good or bad?

I hope this doesn't freak you out, but I sort of used you while I was "having fun."

I imagined her imagining me, and my insides felt crazy.

Maybe this summer we could hang out sometime.

The words grew and shrunk and steadied in my vision. My face burned.

I sort of used you while I was "having fun."

Either I was afraid, or Savannah was so beautiful I couldn't catch my breath. Her long white legs were bare and sandy in her swimsuit. With freckles all over, she was a breathing, running, laughing field of wildflowers. When she kicked up the surf to splash me, I pushed her into a wave, and she dragged me down with her, purple hair sticking to her flushed cheeks and neck.

The ocean swelled, and she pointed out the sea flies. As the foamy water fell back into itself, tiny white creatures rolled across the sand before scurrying back into the ground. When I chased them, Savannah scooped the muddy sand where they disappeared. In her hands, its legs scuttled through the air before she threw it back into the ocean. Then I followed her out into the waves, and we were mermaids together.

That night, we laid on our bellies across her lush, lavender comforter, and she put on a movie that we didn't watch. Instead, we talked about nothing and laughed about everything. I wanted to kiss her so bad, but I was too scared. So I memorized the color of her eyes—blue, with two brown nebulas exploding from the center of each iris.

"It's three in the morning," she finally said.

"Are you tired?" *Please say no.*

"I don't know," she smiled, giggling into her pillow. "Are you?"

"Yeah," I said, my heart pounding. "But I'm not ready to go to sleep."

"Why not?"

"I don't know," I lied. She was so pretty. We were lying in her bed, facing one another, and I wanted so badly to reach out and touch her hand. Her arm. The curve of her hip. But I didn't. For a thousand years, we stayed frozen in that moment, the movie long over, in silence. Breathing.

"Have you ever kissed a girl?" she finally whispered, and I shook my head.

"Have you?"

"No," she said, and I smiled. It was the best no I'd ever heard.

"So—" I stuttered. "So you want to make out with me?"

And then we laughed—the tension broken, her hand reaching up towards my face as she nodded. "Yes." *Yes.*

Her bangs painted my forehead as we kissed for the first time, the sensation of fingernails on my cheeks smearing goosebumps across my collarbone. I could smell her powder—a fragrance so soft and delicate as her skin, burning pale in the darkness of her bedroom.

How innocent we were.

How sweet and fun and pure it was, to make out with Savannah and fall asleep happy.

I spent the night at Savannah's house the next weekend and the weekend after that. Our eyes adjusted to the darkness until the morning light spilled in through the window. At noon, we woke up for breakfast, and her younger sister complained about the owls on the roof, swearing she could hear them all night long.

I wish I could say that was it—that we were the owls, and I was her only secret. We fell in love, and it was the most innocent thing. But there was more to it than that.

Savannah had a boyfriend. She was 17. He was 34, and he was the high school band director. Gary made things complicated. But I shrugged my shoulders when she told me like, *Who cares? We're a secret, too.* Like, maybe I was a new person now outside of the traditional bounds of romance, content with secret, undefined relationships. Maybe I wasn't so serious. Maybe age wasn't as important as I'd thought. I shrugged my shoulders like I believed those things, but really, Gary was too big to think about.

I was tired. I was heartbroken, and Savannah made my insides light up like a goddamn Christmas tree. So, I ignored the obvious: that Gary was a fucking creep.

I met Gary for the first time in the empty hallways of the school.

"It's nice to officially meet you," he smiled, bending down to shake my hand. And I didn't like the way he said "officially," like he'd already heard about me.

"You too," I said, too polite.

He used a ring of keys to open the door to the band room, practically standing in the doorway while ushering us in. They were the same keys Savannah told me they used to fuck in the janitor's closet.

"Step into my office," he smirked.

Then I rushed past the heat of his body, and he closed the door behind us.

"Kind of weird," he said, "that after over a year of dating, you're the only person to ever know about me and Savannah. And I'm the only person who knows about you." His cheeks flushed when he laughed. "Sort of feels like a secret club."

"Yeah," I said, forcing myself to smile.

Did Savannah choose me, or was it Gary?

All that matters, I told myself, *is that he doesn't consider me a threat to their relationship.*

"Are you nervous?" he asked, interrupting my thoughts.

"What—no."

"You're at school. Relax."

Relax. The word echoed in my mind like an alarm disguised as a mantra as Gary led us to the sea of chairs.

The adult picnic game was his idea, and he went first after explaining the rules. "I'm going on a sexy picnic, and I'm bringing anal beads."

Then Savannah. "I'm going on a sexy picnic, and I'm bringing anal beads and…" She paused to think. "Boob jobs."

"I'm going on a sexy picnic," I said, and they burst out laughing.

"What?" I smiled like I was in on the joke.

"She says everything so innocently, doesn't she?" Gary said to Savannah.

"And I'm bringing anal beads, boob jobs, and condoms."

Gary roared with laughter.

Savannah said, "Chloe's too sweet for this game."

"You just don't want to get to D," he raised his eyebrows, and she covered her face with her hands.

"Ew, Gary! No!"

"I'm gonna say it!" he said, tickling her while I watched. Why was I even there? Did Savannah want us all to be friends?

"Gary, No! Don't! It's DISGUSTING!"

"DOUBLE PENETRATION!!!" he shouted, and Savannah groaned. "Fucking gross, dude!"

From his chair, he kicked a cymbal for effect, almost falling over in his giggling.

"She hates it when I say that," he laughed.

"Yep." I figured as much.

Then a janitor poked his head in, saw us and waved. "I'll come back later."

"Let's go somewhere else," Savannah said, and we walked to Gary's car.

From the backseat, I wondered about double penetration. What was it, and why did boys like to see girls squirm? Was it supposed to be hot? I was confused.

Camping with Ezra and his family was like being introduced to religion, a series of rituals, beginning with river baths at sunset. The sky turned to pink lemonade, and I shivered, waist-deep in the cold water. Ezra tossed me a bottle of shampoo from the purple shower caddy on the bank, and I squirted the noxious, artificial-smelling goop into my palm.

Olivia set her yellow razor on a massive tree root, suspended over the river from years of erosion. The ancient tree shaded us from any sun that may have soothed my goosebumps while Nikki and Malik rubbed themselves down with loofahs beside me. Ezra shamelessly put a soapy hand down his shorts, and I dove headfirst into the water with my hair full of suds, swimming against the gentle current.

When I finally washed away all the grime of the past year, I sank my feet into the muddy river bottom and crawled up the bank—lush, dirty tree branches caressing me all the way.

When lightning bugs glittered in the blue darkness, a group of men in dirty white t-shirts sat on upturned gallon buckets, playing soft bluegrass music over the sounds of crickets and bullfrogs. The light of the fire cast an orange glow upon the backs of the small crowd forming, as they patted their legs to the rhythm of the music—banjos, guitars, and gentle choruses. How mesmerizing it was, to watch country men be vulnerable, stringing beauty out of thin air as camp carried on around them. Then the bugs started nipping—black flying insects that had me ruffling my hair, convinced that I could feel them crawling, and us kids took shelter in Ezra's tent.

Between the nylon walls, Ezra switched on the hanging lantern as we piled in between the cots. Covered in a film of bug spray and campfire, we sat on sleeping bags and pillows with Malik's little cousin and the Game of Life on the floor between us. But even though we all went to college, Ezra picked the doctor card first.

"Fuck you," Malik said, chugging a Mountain Dew.

"Bitch, I *earned this.*"

"Ezra, do you know how many *years*—" Malik began.

"Yes, and OBVIOUSLY I did the time because I have the doctor card and you don't, so stuff it, Dew boy!" Then he moved his car seven spaces and shouted, "Yay! Payday!" And Nikki begrudgingly gave him a hundred thousand dollars from the bank.

When it was time to get married, Ezra chose Jeremy from Paramore, even though I knew he'd rather be with Nikki.

Malik handed me a blue person on my turn, and I told him to give me a pink instead.

"Chloe's fucking a girl right now," Ezra clarified.

"She's the coolest," I added.

Nikki sulked, "I wish I was fucking a girl."

He and Malik picked hot female celebrities. Ezra rolled his eyes, and then it was Malik's cousin's turn.

Brandon stared at the board with his elbows on his knees—his deadpan face glowing in the concentrated light of the lantern, but he was silent.

"Zac Efron," he said finally, moving only his lips.

"Really?" I asked. "Cool."

Malik and Nikki froze.

Ezra shouted, "You heard the man! Give him a blue!"

"No, no, wait!" Brandon yelled, bursting to life again as Nikki fumbled with the pieces. "Megan Fox! I want Megan Fox!"

"Damn—another false victory for the Gay Agenda."

I floated the river in a green kayak, dipping my fingers into the water, creating patterns both visual and tactile, and I let myself forget. I couldn't hold it anymore—my parents, Savannah, Gary. The sun's rays sank deep into my bones, burning off the weight in my chest.

I'll never forget Ezra in his black sunglasses and puffy palm tree swim trunks—the yellow bandana tied around his greasy river hair. His smile was my liberation that year, as he led us down the river in his flaming red kayak, with a cow skull on the bow and an American flag rippling in the wind behind him.

At home, in a land far, far away, Mom organized the Exodus—didn't touch a damn box. She made Dad do everything. Then she sat on the floor of their empty bedroom and cried before walking into her new home with everything in its place.

On the river, I jumped into the rapids and screamed laughing. A pair of mating dragonflies landed on Malik's nose, and the female arched its back to create a heart.

Mom welcomed herself into single motherhood.

On the drive back to Virginia Beach, I felt that I was on my way to a new life. All I had was an address that brought me to a row of townhouses painted in coastal shades of white, gray, and blue. The fixtures over the doorways—arches or curly French mustaches—were the same color as the shutters. As I parked the car, I hoped that I was in the right place—and that ours was one of the pastel blue buildings with the mustaches.

But when I called her, she didn't pick up. Instead, she appeared outside the door of an off-white building with a navy-blue arch over the door. Like a little kid, she put her hands over her mouth in excitement, and I burst from the car.

We crashed into a hug, and I screamed.

"It's perfect!" I told her. Then we walked arm in arm, giggly with excitement, down a skinny concrete path that led directly to the front door of our new home.

Inside, the living room's cream carpet stretched far and wide, opening up into a tiny kitchen with white tiles. The couch and dark cherry furniture looked better than it ever had in the old house, and upstairs, our bedrooms waited with blank walls and familiar comforters on the beds—my parents', with black and white ruffles, and mine. As soon as I saw it, I threw myself onto the orange polka dots, lying back and staring up at the ceiling.

"It's not perfect," Mom said, and I interrupted her.

"Yes, it is." She sat down beside me, and I was so relieved. I didn't have to watch it anymore—the disintegration of my parents' relationship. I didn't have to think about it or know about it. I could just be me.

"Okay," she smiled, squeezing my hand. "It's perfect."

The next night, Dad picked me up in his red pickup truck. We were driving somewhere I'd never been before. My body was smashed against the passenger door, and I didn't know what to say.

"You don't have to feel awkward. It doesn't have to be awkward at all," he said, eyes glazed with sadness, and I shrugged. It was anyway.

He parked in a dark empty lot, and even though I couldn't see it, I knew when I stepped out of the truck that we were at the ocean. The waves crashed in my ears as we slowly made our way towards the sand. The moon was bright on the blowing reeds, and even though it was still summer, the air was chilly. My dad's mouth was a straight line of worry, and I felt the same way. Where was our easy togetherness? Was it gone forever?

Some nights are too sad to remember.

When I was five, Dad took me to watch the sea turtles hatch on the Outer Banks. There was a mountain of eggs half-buried in the hole their mother had carved out for them, tucked in like a womb in the sand. Yellow tape blocked the crowd from getting too close. But we were lucky, Dad said, that it was a full moon. Because when the turtles hatched, we were going to see everything. But even though we waited for hours and didn't use our flashlights and were patient the whole time, nothing happened. The sea turtles never hatched, and Dad carried me home while I cried.

It was the same week I fell in love with the ocean. I wore a blue life jacket with purple straps, and every day, Dad took me out to the water. He held my hand while I jumped over the waves, lifting me so high above the surf that I squealed laughing.

In the shallow, I sat on his lap, and when the big waves came, he took huge, dramatic breaths, puffing his cheeks and letting the water pull him under. His head and torso were blurry in the waves, with sand and seashells swirling all around him. Then he burst through the surface, my dad in the world again, gasping for air, and I laughed and laughed. I loved him so much.

Mom left Dad the ugly red loveseat and the TV.

Dad bought a record player and a dog.

Savannah and I knelt on the floor of my old kitchen, and I smelled Max's sweet puppy breath for the first time. I scratched his velvet belly, ignoring Dad and pretending everything was normal. Dad put his hands on his hips and forced a laugh.

"Do you like him?" he asked.

"Duh." What kind of question was that? "Let's play a game or something."

He looked over his shoulder at the new folding table, piled high with junk—backpacks, jackets, camping gear, mail. Then he walked out of the kitchen and came back with a piece of plywood.

"This should do it," Dad grunted, laying it across the top of two chairs. He put Johnny Cash's prison album on the record player, and as the three of us played Monopoly on the makeshift table, I thought that maybe the bachelor life suited him.

That night, Savannah spent the night at the townhouse. Mom was out with a friend from work, and we had the house to ourselves—the luxury of making out in the living room and jumping on the couch, blasting our favorite music.

"I'm so glad you're not a guy," I laughed. "This would never happen."

It was the ultimate sleepover until the doorknob started jiggling, and Mom's friend walked into the house without her.

"Where's Mom?" I asked, pausing the music.

"Girls," she began, pushing her hair behind her ears. She was tall and robust, slow and careful with her words. "Amber has had a little too much to drink, and she's embarrassed."

She paused.

"Where's my mom?" I asked again.

"Why don't you two step into the bathroom while I get her upstairs."

"Fine."

Savannah and I stood with our ears pressed against the bathroom door.

"Is she okay?" Savannah whispered, but I put my finger to my lips. Like I just wanted to hear the front door open—keys clinking in their purses, clothes shuffling up the narrow townhouse stairs. Like I didn't need Savannah to shut up for just one more minute while I tried to get over my mom's limp body being dragged up the stairs.

Like I wasn't scared, as I silently turned the doorknob and tiptoed out of the bathroom.

"What are you doing?" Savannah followed, and I didn't answer her.

"Why are you being so quiet?" she whispered, as I sat down on the couch, and I shrugged. *I don't know.*

Soft footsteps thud down the stairs until the woman stood in the doorway again.

"I thought you were in the bathroom," she said, and then she left.

In the morning, there were stories. Mom and the woman—Michelle—in the back of a car with two strange men up front. Mom thought she'd lost her phone, but when

Michelle called her number, it started ringing from the front of the car. The men started laughing, and Mom and Michelle were scared. Mom wondered out loud which one of them had drugged her.

"I don't want you over there all the time," Mom told me. Our house… Dad's house now, was only a few miles away, and at first, she'd done it on purpose. I hadn't seen him in weeks anyway.

"I want him to feel the emptiness," she said, and I took notes in my head. Would the emptiness bring Dad back? I just wanted my mom to be happy.

Another time, she said, "I want you to be able to see us both equally," and I smiled.

"I know, Mom."

"I just want him to feel better," she said. But her voice cracked, and she disappeared into her room. Sometimes, I wanted to cry over her sadness, but if I were caught, she might feel guilty—and what if she told Dad, and then he felt guilty? So, I didn't cry, even when I was home alone. Because what if she got off work early? Or what if I couldn't stop? Or my eyes were puffy, and I had nothing to blame it on? What if my sadness made her even more sad?

Conversations with Mom:

"Can I get my nose pierced?"
"No."

"Can I shave my head?"
"No."

I hated that word, which was the opposite of freedom—which was my life, narrowing down on me—putting me into boxes that I never agreed to be in. I wanted to feel the wind on my neck. I wanted three-minute showers—sleeping in until the last minute. How would it feel to be beautiful without my hair? To see my face better—to know the shape of my head.

"Why won't you let me?" I whined. I showed her pictures of Natalie Portman. She was so beautiful.

"How about—we get your nose pierced instead?" she asked.

I started cutting my hair in my bedroom with the door closed. With the dirty, full-length mirror set up against the dresser, I'd reach for the paper scissors whenever I wanted to transform. With each cut, the scissors made a ripping noise. My hair fell in chunks, dispersing into a million indistinguishable pieces. I trimmed my dead ends, and I felt new. I gave myself bangs. I brought my hair up past my shoulders and looked exactly how I felt. Messy and distorted. Chopped and layered in a bad way.

Mom met a man named Jack on the internet.

"I'm almost a hundred percent sure he's gay," she told me. Sitting by the fireplace in his home, he read her a story, which was endearing except, "He told the story like I was in actual kindergarten," she said. "It was kind of *awkward.*" And then the kiss—a closed mouth, dispassionate event that made my heart sink to the bottom floor of the house and beyond. She kissed him—a gay man with whom she had no chemistry. She'd kissed him anyway. She kissed a bad kisser.

I couldn't talk for an hour after she told me.

"Did you think I wouldn't kiss anyone?" she asked, and I guess I didn't.

"I don't know."

When Mom said she was going out with a friend, she was too casual.

"Okay," I said, feigning indifference. But what did that even mean? Was it actually a friend, or was she going on a date? Did I even care?

"Great!" she smiled. "He'll be here in an hour."

The friend picked Mom up with a bouquet of yellow roses, which was apparently the color of friendship but also her favorite color. Inside, he sat on the couch, his biceps bulging out of his shirt as he stumbled over his words.

"Check this out," he said. "I got a new tattoo yesterday." He opened his arm to show me the inside of his elbow. "I've wanted this tattoo my whole life."

It was an open razor blade, with the handle on his forearm and the sharp edge slicing into his bicep. A drop of blood spilled out onto his skin. "And when I bend my arm," he said, "it cuts."

"What does it mean?" I asked, my voice flat.

Nothing.

"What?" he said.

It meant nothing.

Savannah was my first kiss and my first time falling in love with a girl. She was my first undefined relationship and the first one I ever hid from my parents. Why tell them, when we could do whatever we wanted? When no one suspected?

But there were other reasons. Like the time I told Mom I thought I might be bi, and she said that a lot of girls go through that phase. That it was normal to be confused. She didn't get it.

What would I have said, anyway? That I had a girlfriend? I didn't. That I was falling in love through a constellation of intimate moments centered around Savannah? That me and my "new best friend" were finger-banging every night? Yeah, that would have gone well. Especially when I told them about Gary. That would have gone really, really well.

Savannah and I made out in the back of Gary's car while he complained about his landlord. She'd pull her face away just long enough to say, "Uh-huh," and I'd hold in my laughter, feeling it all the way down my spine.

But in the end, I wanted more than our secret giggling. I wanted proof that she felt the same way I did—that I was more than just a bi-curious experiment. I wanted to be her girlfriend. I wanted to tell people about us. I wanted Gary out of the picture and so much more. Ease. Fearlessness. Exquisite simplicity. I wanted a love that was liberating.

But the day I made Savannah choose between me and Gary, she never looked at me the same. Never smiled again so easily. I already knew who she was going to pick anyway. Not me. And honestly, it was better that way. Because as soon as she chose him, I could pry myself away from her. I didn't expect her to talk about it with him. I didn't expect her to come back with a plan of her own.

Savannah chose me, after talking with him, because he would wait for her if it didn't work out. She didn't hug me when she said it. She didn't smile or even look at me, and it was all wrong. There was no way we were going to work out. Because now, she was heartbroken. Now, she resented me.

Those last few weeks in September, the crisp air turned her cheeks bright pink. The wind whipped her hair across her face, and she held it back while I put red lipstick on her. Then she kissed me, sitting on a park bench, smearing red across my face. It was the only time we kissed in public, and I was in love in the most horrible way.

I broke up with her over the phone, and I exploded. All of my anger—from everything. She sobbed, as the rage flooded through my veins—boiling, exhilarating rage.

I screamed, "GO—FUCK—GARY!" Then I hung up the phone, and I felt energized—and in control of something.

Being a teenager felt like being pushed out of a plane and screaming bloody murder as I flailed through the air, catching fire in the atmosphere. In my mind, I'd never make it past 23. I couldn't imagine surviving it.

We had hair dye parties at Ezra's house, and sometimes, when my hair was green, I could convince myself that I'd jumped from the plane on purpose, and I didn't know what I wanted more—to be in the plane or on the ground. Most of the time, I imagined myself midair, halfway between the two, holding onto my limbs, eyes cinched shut, and all I could hope for was to land in water.

Sometimes, late at night, we'd take turns telling secrets— the Secret Game. And in that way, we bound ourselves to each other. For Malik, it was the image he saw, every time he closed his eyes. A wall of bricks. He had dreams about it crumbling, and nightmares where he pounded it, or it caved in on him, and he woke up shaking.

When Ezra was little, he had an alter ego like a superhero inside his head. Her name was Jessie, and out here in the country, where being gay was considered a sin, she made life more bearable. When he couldn't hold the weight, she held the parts of him that were forbidden.

It felt good to know that if I ever lost myself, they could pull me back in. They could remind me who I was, and in turn, I'd be their Horcrux. I held their secrets in my heart be- cause they made my life less terrifying. As we drove across counties, just to listen to the music with the windows down, my friends made falling to my own imminent death more whimsical. We had homework parties where we laughed more than we worked, and there was always, always Gaga.

Our first time watching the *Marry the Night* music video, Ezra painted a blue lightning bolt over his eye. Olivia wore a black bandana with the floating eyeliner from the *Judas* music video, and I was *Americana,* with Captain America boxers, a blue tank top, and an American flag bandana.

We'd been dancing all night under the light of the cranking disco ball. Now, as Ezra set up the projector, we sat on the floor in reverence. When Ezra pressed play, Lady Gaga's bare face stretched across the wall like a movie theatre. No music. Just her monotone voice in an epic monologue.

Until that night, I'd only liked Lady Gaga because Ezra did. Now, as I listened to her speak on trauma, memories, and reinventing the past, I finally understood why she meant so much to him. Ezra cried, the tears flowing seamlessly over his makeup. Lady Gaga was pushed into the hospital wing on a stretcher, and I wished that this could all be part of a past that I was reinventing. That one day, I would be able to make sense of my life in a way that felt both beautiful and meaningful.

In the middle of the night, when Ezra's parents were asleep, we snuck outside with a gallon of milk and a box of Honey Nut Cheerios to reenact the second part of the story. In an old shed with a gravel floor, we listened to the song again—dancing our hearts out and ripping off our clothes, pouring milk and Cheerios over our naked bodies. When the song was over and everything was quiet, we looked at each other, soaking wet, with cereal stuck to our skin, and laughed. Then I sat on the ground in nothing but boxers and a bandana and ate Cheerios out of the gravel while Ezra ran inside for towels. I was officially a Little Monster.

PART III

Age 25

Without home or family, Mom followed her childhood dreams of becoming a flight attendant and escaped into the clouds. Every once in a while, I got lucky, and the airline paid for her to spend the night in Richmond.

"Hi, Butterfly!" she squealed, reaching towards me in her red lipstick and short black heels. In her room, she changed into her pajamas, and we sat together on one of the beds, leaning back against a mountain of fluffy pillows.

"I have something for youuu," she sang into the silence. "Look in my makeup bag."

On the second bed, in the pile of her stunning, vagrant life, was a black nylon pouch. Inside, I found a keychain—a rocket ship bedazzled with blue and silver sequins. "I got it on one of my trips to Huntsville, in Alabama!" she said. "They're really into NASA for some reason." She was forever thinking about me, adding to my collection of sentimental shrapnel.

As I twisted the ring onto my car keys, she rummaged through her purse.

"What I really wanted to give you is in here," she said, handing me a small velvet bag that reminded me of picking through rocks in souvenir shops. Feeling the material between my fingers, I felt the outline of a ring and stopped.

The year before, when she'd caught me staring at her hand, she shrugged and scrunched her nose. "Sometimes I wear it when I feel lonely." Edges of gold clasped the trillion-cut diamond in place. Now, through the bag, the diamond was smooth like water. I hugged her tight as she said softly, "It doesn't look like I'll be needing it any time soon."

I took my own wedding ring off, a thick silver band with a single emerald stud, and I slid the diamond ring around my finger—my hands, no longer mine, but familiar. I'd seen them before from the passenger's seat of the car—when else were my mother's hands on display? —on the steering wheel, driving down the interstate, sunlight glinting off the multifaceted stone. And beside me, folded into her lap, were ten tan, wrinkling fingers. The hands of a woman almost fifty.

Her face smiled, crinkling slightly in this aged version of herself. "You'll give it new life," she said, soon growing sleepy and sinking into the bed.

On the drive home, my left hand rested at eleven o'clock, moving slightly with the curves in the road, while the other worked the stick. The ring slipped backwards as the stone pressed into the soft underside of my finger. I fixed it, and it spun again, and then later after parking in the driveway and pushing down the gray manual lock, slamming the door shut behind me.

"Did it do this when you wore it?" I'd asked her at the hotel, and she'd smiled, a girl in love.

"Yeah, but I didn't mind." I imagined the nuisance like a mindfulness bell, constant reminders throughout her day. *You're loved. You're safe. You're happy.*

I had the feeling that she'd finally given up her mantra, passing the pain onto me to transform. From my hands pulsed the weight of an intricate grief, tied up in the hope of holding on and the deep suffering of letting go. Not just hers, but mine. Our stories are linked in the family we once shared, the trauma of losing the essential third of the Tripod.

The year before the fracture, I bought an astrology book, meticulously mapping out the sky of the night I was born—the position of the sun, moon, and planets; the constellations, ever-abstract to my unskilled eyes, of the astrological signs on the horizon.

Who am I? I'd asked, and it told me. And then I outlined my parents' skies, struck by a similarity in all three of our birth charts—a North Node in Sagittarius—the point at which the lines of the moon and the sun's orbits cross paths on the night we were born. The North Node has been described by astrologers as the blueprint of the soul, and it became apparent to me on that night that the three of us—Mom, Dad, and I—were predestined to be together—our life's purpose, all tied up in one another like energetic star paths, glittering gold beneath the surface of the seeable universe.

Dad doesn't talk about it anymore, but Mom and I, we held on, welded in our hope, both real and habitual, that Dad would come back to us. I see the absurdity of this thinking on my end. How much would it really affect me, a married woman, if my parents got back together? But the philosopher in me needs to know: Can what is pure be repaired? Love and marriage. My mom's broken heart.

Now I'm 25, and in love with my husband in a way I had started doubting was possible. *Happy Anniversary,* Mom wrote on this year's Hallmark card. *You and Matthew remind me of me and Dad.* It's the best compliment, a love I'd always dreamed for myself. And in that, there is hope, and there is fear.

The day of our third wedding anniversary, Matthew and I closed on our first house together. Our last night in the apartment, I took pictures of the masking tape labels over the towel hooks in the bathroom. A year ago, he'd written our names in Sharpie so that I would never wipe toothpaste off my mouth with the wrong towel again.

Now, he was watching Netflix in bed with his head propped up on a pillow. I sat down next to him, curling my legs against his body. He paused the show to meet my gaze as I looked at him with the eyes of a thousand memories.

"We're becoming such a family," I said softly.

"What do you mean?" he asked.

"We've been married for almost three years. We have a house." I paused. "We'll have kids."

He searched my face thoughtfully for the meaning behind my words.

"It's scary," I confessed, my heart ripping in half.

"What's scary about it?" he asked, taking my hand, and what I said surprised me.

"Things just end."

"What do you mean?"

"The more stable we get, somehow, the scarier it is."

"You mean the longer we're together, the closer we are to breaking up." The confusion on his face cleared.

"Yeah," I said, pulling my sweater up over my cheeks as the tears surged down my red, blotchy face.

"Chloe, I love you," he said. "I'll never leave you."

"You don't know, Matthew. Things just end! Everything's fine and then it's not and there's no way to prepare for any of it! You just stop loving me!" My hands hovered, open and frantic, inches from my face.

"I'll never stop loving you, Chloe." His voice was hurt, but I wasn't hearing him anymore.

"Chloe, breathe," he said, and I realized that I was hyperventilating. I put my feet on the ground and held my stomach.

Then I focused my attention on forcing air through my constricted throat while Matthew rubbed my back. With my breath, I worked to unclench the tight knot I'd woven into my abdomen. Even as the last of my tears seeped out, I wiped the wetness from my cheeks, feeling my eyelashes on the tops of my eyelids like wet paintbrushes.

I smiled softly at my husband. "Sorry," I said, and he hugged me tight. In these ways, I let go, both of us understanding why and where it came from.

The ring floats around the house now. I smudged it, in the new house, with the small bundle of burnt white sage that sits on the windowsill above the kitchen sink. Then I left it to rest on the spike of a large amethyst crystal that lives in the bathroom, with a vision of sadness seeping out like oil, black and pungent. And then, onto the stone tiles beside the toilet, I fell to my knees and cried on the floor, doubled over and alone, at last, far enough removed to feel my own grief, tucked away for a day like today—spacious and unassuming.

A few months have passed, and the ring sits with my heirloom jewelry. I honor it as a relic amongst late grandmothers' intricate wedding bands, a smattering of turquoise, and a turtle pin from my mother-in-law, her wedding gift to me—"something old." On days I'm feeling utilitarian, I put my mom's ring on display in the glass, gold-rimmed case that holds my collection of crystals—a diamond by definition.

I'm letting go of the idea that my fate is tied into my parents', or theirs into mine. And I'm realizing that the possibility of true, forever love can't be proven. It's too much pressure, for me and for him. We deserve to be taken off the pedestal, our humanness appreciated in its entirety. Still, sometimes I wear the ring. Not for remembering, but because it's pretty. I

like the way the light bounces off the surface, a visual orches-
tra, so blatant in my love—free from expectations, permission
to be imperfect.

About the Author

Haylee Manda Reynolds lives in Indianapolis with her heavy metal husband and geriatric guinea pig, Poppy. She enjoys going on adventures, discovering new swimming holes, writing, and making zines.

More of her work can be found in *Buddhist Poetry Review*, *HerWords* literary magazine, *the Closed Eye Open*, and *Losing Friends Underwater*, a zine of poetry and underwater disposable photography.

This is her debut novel.

Acknowledgments

Thank you, Mom, for reading every draft and being my biggest cheerleader. Your brightness, positivity, and belief in me carried me through the process of bringing this story to life.

Shoutout to my dads for supporting me in everything I do—for teaching me to climb rooftops and jump cliffs, and for encouraging me to follow my dreams.

Josee, you're such a badass. Thanks for being the best sister in the world and for insisting that I keep trying when I almost gave up on publishing. I hope you have no difficulty finding yourself written into the characters in Chloe's life.

My utmost gratitude to Susie, Aaron, Blaire, Marian, and especially Stella Sharples, who shared her writing with me and asked to see mine. Stella, thank you for asking to read more about Rory, for screening my chapters for cheesiness, and for insisting that I publish this dang book already so you and your friends can read it. You have no idea how much joy and confidence your interest has brought me.

Erin Roberts, I love you. Thank you for reading my draft at Max Patch and being the first person to read my book for pleasure.

Eternal gratitude to my Aunt Charlene, for cultivating the writer in me since elementary school; to Beanie, for being my

number one fan; and to the rest of my family, for your uncon-
ditional love and support.

Victoria Fann, I'll always appreciate you for leading the
women's writing group that birthed this project. Stephanie,
Sue, Rachel, Annie, Jackie, and Laura, thank you for your wisdom, kindness, and feedback, and for being a safe space to
share my shitty art. Your stories will live in my heart forever.

Most of all, Aaron, thank you for reading every draft, for
finding the right moments to give me difficult feedback, and
for being my partner and fellow artist in this life, my soulmate
who understands every nook and cranny of the artmaking
process—from the thrill of creation to the demoralizing slog
of getting it out into the world. Your love, silliness, and wisdom mean everything to me.

For those I didn't mention, you know who you are. Thank
you for the years of hysterical laughter. My life was meaning-
less before you.

www.ingramcontent.com/pod-product-compliance
Lightning Source LLC
Chambersburg PA
CBHW031250210726
48287CB00003B/975